Better than Ellie

I think of how Ellie can do everything better than me—even following directions—and how she's always quiet even when she's supposed to be. And then I remember that she's quiet even when she doesn't have to be. She's kind of shy. I feel a happy ping inside of me. Quiet Ellie up on stage? In front of all those people? Her?

And suddenly I know absolutely positively with sugar on top that I've found the thing that I'll be better at than Ellie. I've found the thing that will make Mr. Mooney like me better than he likes her. I will be the star of his play. I will be Cinderella! In my mind, I can already see myself onstage taking a bow. I can hear everyone clapping for me, me, me! My mom and dad and JT are all in the audience (not Liza, though, because she'd cry and spoil it), clapping. Best of all, Mr. Mooney is backstage, beaming a big smile at me so bright it's like a spotlight, lighting me up onstage.

OTHER BOOKS YOU MAY ENJOY

Mary Margaret,
Center Stage

Christine Kole MacLean

PUFFIN BOOKS

PUFFIN BOOKS

Published by the Penguin Group

Penguin Young Readers Group, 345 Hudson Street, New York, New York 10014, U.S.A.

Penguin Group (Canada), 90 Eglinton Avenue, Suite 700,

Toronto, Ontario, Canada M4P 2Y3 (a division of Pearson Penguin Canada Inc.)

Penguin Books Ltd, 80 Strand, London WC2R 0RL, England

Penguin Ireland, 25 St Stephen's Green, Dublin 2, Ireland

(a division of Penguin Books Ltd)

Penguin Group (Australia), 250 Camberwell Road, Camberwell, Victoria 3124, Australia

(a division of Pearson Australia Group Pty Ltd)

Penguin Books India Pvt Ltd, 11 Community Centre, Panchsheel Park,

New Delhi - 110 017, India

Penguin Group (NZ), Cnr Airborne and Rosedale Roads,

Albany, Auckland 1310, New Zealand (a division of Pearson New Zealand Ltd)

Penguin Books (South Africa) (Pty) Ltd, 24 Sturdee Avenue,

Rosebank, Johannesburg 2196, South Africa

Registered Offices: Penguin Books Ltd, 80 Strand, London WC2R 0RL, England

First published in the United States of America by Dutton Children's Books,
a division of Penguin Young Readers Group, 2006
Published by Puffin Books, a division of Penguin Young Readers Group, 2007

1 3 5 7 9 10 8 6 4 2

THE LIBRARY OF CONGRESS HAS CATALOGED THE DUTTON CHILDREN'S BOOKS EDITION AS FOLLOWS:

MacLean, Christine Kole.

Mary Margaret, center stage / by Christine Kole MacLean. — 1st ed.

p.   cm.

Summary: Mary Margaret is hoping to be Cinderella in the community play but
must face the fact that the lead will be played by Ellie, the new girl in class
who seems to do everything right.

ISBN 0-525-47597-4 (hardcover)

[1. Self-perception—Fiction. 2. Interpersonal relations—Fiction.
3. Theater—Fiction.] I. Title.

PZ7.M22423Marc 2006

[Fic]—dc22   2005009093

Puffin Books ISBN 978-0-14-240768-4

Designed by Irene Vandevoort.

Printed in the United States of America

To Steph Owens Lurie—Cheers!

Acknowledgments

Special thanks to those who helped shape this book in ways
large and small: Michelle Bombe, Lois Maassen, Jodi Zenk
and the entire cast and crew of the Holland Civic
Theatre's 2004 production of *The Spell of Sleeping Beauty*,
Danielle ("Veruca Salt") Schmidt, Bill Bryson, Sharon Dwyer,
and (as always)
Clark MacLean and Madeline MacLean.

Contents

Mary Margaret,

Center Stage

P eople! People! Listen up!" Mr. Mooney says. Out of the corner of my eye I see that he's waving hand-outs over his head, but the rest of my eye I'm keep-ing on Ellie. She is the team leader for her group. I am the team leader for my group. There are four other team leaders, too, but I don't care about them. I only care about me and Ellie, my team and her team—especially about my team beating her team. Ellie is sitting all quiet, looking up at Mr. Mooney like she's a trained dog waiting for her owner to give the next command. I squinch my eyes at her. Roll over! I think. Sit! Stay!

"Mary Margaret, what are we supposed to be doing?" Kyle says. I know it's Kyle without even looking at him, because he always talks like he has a cold. "Sit!" I hiss, still looking at Ellie. "Stay!"

Kyle sits.

"This is a quiz about following instructions and work-ing as a team," Mr. Mooney says, handing out the sheets and a brown paper bag at each table. "Do *not* open the bag. Team leaders for the week—you're responsible for helping your team do the best possible job." When Mr. Mooney gets to our table, he puts both his hands on my desk and leans over me. "This is not a contest. This is not about who gets done first." He says it loud like he is telling the whole class, but he is looking right into my eyes.

Mr. Mooney is pretty smart. He's the one who told us that it's better to be last through the lunch line than first, because the lunch ladies will give the last class leftover cookies, if you make sad eyes at them and ask very sweetly. And he knows that when the computer isn't working right, it's because it got up on the wrong side of bed, and if you give it another chance by turning it off and then on again, lots of times it will get up on the *right* side of bed. Best of all, on the first day of school, before I even had a chance to tell him, he knew that I had just had a birthday. So he's right about a lot of things. But he's wrong about the quiz not being a contest. For a girl like me who has a girl like Ellie sitting two groups away, *everything* is a contest.

Mr. Mooney is still looking at me. I smile to show him that I am listening. He moves on to the next group. Because Mr. Mooney stopped at Ellie's group first, my group is already behind. I snatch up the piece of paper and begin reading. I am reading so hard that when he says, "Take your time. The first instruction is to read all the instructions care-fully," his voice sounds far away, like my mother's when we're at the beach and she calls to me and I almost don't hear her because of the waves and the wind.

1. Read all the instructions.

Okay, that's easy enough. I look around. Everyone is still reading.

2. Using a number-two pencil, write out the first names of everyone in your group in alphabetical order.

By now I can hear Collin's group arguing about what number the lead in his mechanical pencil is, so I know they have already started doing the things on the sheet. I scoot up to the edge of my seat. Sitting on the edge of my seat is sort of like a shortcut to working good and fast.

3. Choose one person from your group to be the listener. Give that person a piece of paper and a pencil and have her turn her back to the rest of the team. The other team members may look to see what's in the bag. Now, without naming the object, tell the person how to draw it, step by step.

By now, almost all the groups have begun working, and we are even further behind. I am too antsy to read any more. "Let's just start," I say.

"It says to read all the instructions," says Brett, looking over at Ellie's group.

"But everyone is getting ahead of us!" I say.

McKenzie crosses her arms over her chest. "You're supposed to be the leader, Mary Margaret, remember? And leaders help people *always* do the right thing. That's what Mr. Mooney says." Brett nods. Kyle just sits. I clamp my teeth together and decide I'll just have to read faster.

4. *Arrange the people in your group from tallest to short-est. Go to step 5.*

5. *Tie your right leg to the left leg of the person stand-ing next to you, using the yarn in the bag. Use the yarn colors in the order that they appear in a rainbow and*

"Forget it!" I say, slapping the instructions down and grabbing a pencil. "Alphabetical order for our group is . . ." I look around. "Brett, Kyle . . ."

"But you haven't read all the way through," says McKenzie. "And leaders *always*—"

"Win," I say.

Brett frowns. "I don't think Mr. Mooney ever said that."

"Let's take a vote," says McKenzie.

This is not going so good. I can hear a paper bag crin-kle somewhere near where Ellie's group is sitting, so at least one group is already on step three. If we don't start right now, we'll never catch up. It may already be too late! "Kyle," I say, "do you want to be a loser?" Kyle doesn't say anything. "Speak!" I say.

He points his nose up to the ceiling like a dog howl-ing at the moon. "I don't want to be a loser," he says.

I look at Brett. Just then his stomach growls, which gives me an idea. "I'll give you my bag of chips at lunch," I say.

He shrugs. "Okay."

The vote is three to one. Right away McKenzie slows

us down on step two by arguing that *McKenzie* comes before *Mary Margaret* in the alphabet. She's doing it on purpose because she's mad that she lost the vote. All she wants is to get her own way. She wouldn't make a good leader because leaders are supposed to think about everyone and not just themselves.

Kyle is good at following directions (he's still sitting), so we decide he'll be the one to do the drawing on the third step. He turns his back, and the rest of us jump up and peek inside the bag. We get lucky this time. It's just a square, so telling him how to draw it will be easy.

"Draw four lines," Brett says. Kyle draws four lines all different lengths and all bunched together, like he's drawing the legs of a cat.

"No!" we all shout at the same time.

"Draw two lines the same size a little way apart," I say. Kyle does. "Now draw two more lines that connect everything." Kyle does.

"Oh!" he says, all glad. "We had an M in our bag!"

"You're not doing it right," I say. "You have to listen!" Behind us, I hear some kids fighting about whether the colors of the rainbow are ROY G. BIV or ROY B. GIV, which means they are already on step four. The only good news about that is that it's not Ellie's group.

Kyle stamps his foot. "I did just what you said," he says. "You're not telling me right!"

McKenzie elbows me out of the way so she's next to Kyle. "I'll do it," she says.

I don't know why she thinks she can when she didn't even know that *Mary Margaret* comes before *McKenzie* in the alphabet. "What makes you think you're so smart?" I ask.

She taps her head. "Because I've been using this, that's why," she says, like she *invented* thinking. "Kyle, do it again. This time draw two lines up and down a little ways apart." She watches Kyle as he draws and then yells, "The same length! Make them the same length." Kyle does. "Now draw a line that connects the top of those two lines . . ." She waits for him to catch up. "And a line that connects the bottom of those two lines.

"There," McKenzie says, all proud of herself.

"It's a rectangle," I say. "You didn't tell him that all four lines need to be the same length." Finally, Kyle draws it right.

"All that for a dumb square?" he asks.

I'm already pulling the yarn out of our bag for step four. When I look up to see who is taller, McKenzie or Brett, I see that Ellie's group is just sitting there, watching everyone else in the class. It looks to me like they haven't even started yet, and this fills me up with happiness. "Quick! Line up shortest to tallest," I say, thinking *Roy G. Biv, Roy G. Biv*, and laying the yarn out: Red! Orange! Yellow! Green! Got it! We do that step fast.

For the sixth thing, we're supposed to march backwards to the principal's office singing, "Heigh-ho, heigh-ho, it's off to work we go." That's a little weird, but that's what step six says, and it's a test on following directions, so we do it. By now, we are way ahead of everyone else, and there's only one step left before we win. Ellie is still just sitting there watching everyone. Eat my dust, I think. My brother JT says he thinks that every time he pulls ahead of another runner during a race.

We have to turn the page over to read the last step. When I read it, my mouth flops open. The last step can't be right! I read it again. And again, because my dad always says the third time is the charm. Too bad that this time it isn't. Because the last direction is

6. *Ignore all the other directions before this one. Sit quietly at your tables until Mr. Mooney says the test is over.*

I stare up at Mr. Mooney, who is raining down his "good job" smile on Ellie's table. It is my very favorite Mr. Mooney smile—except for when he beams it on Ellie, like he is doing now. Like he did when she passed level 15 in math, while everyone else was still on level 13. And like he did last week after the fall spelling bee, when Ellie beat me on *occasionally*. Someone must have changed the spelling of that dumb word since I learned it last year, because suddenly it had only one *s*. So far she is better than me at math, spelling, reading, and social studies. And now this.

Now she's even better than me at following directions.

For the bazillionth time since Ellie moved here and joined our class, it's me who is eating Ellie's dust. And it doesn't taste that good.

"So you don't like the new girl?" Andy asks me on the bus ride home. I have been trying to tell him how Ellie is ruining school for me. Andy is my best friend from summer vacation. I got to know him through his dog, Itzy, who is named for some famous violin player. We aren't in the same class, but we sit together on the bus and compare the best and worst things that happened at school.

I think about whether or not I like Ellie while I give Stevie Butts a cookie from my lunch. I always give him a cookie from my lunch because I feel sorry for him. Nobody ever calls him Stevie. It's always Stevie Butts. Out on the playground, kids will yell, "Stevie Butts, you get back here!" and "It's Stevie Butts's turn on the climbing wall." I'd like to give him a new last name, but I can't. So I give him a cookie.

"A sugar cookie today?" he says. "I love sugar. Thanks, Mary Margaret!"

"You're welcome, Stevie Butts," I say, out of habit. I turn around in my seat and say to Andy, "I don't like Ellie, but I don't *not* like her, either."

Andy flaps the end of his tie like it's a wing. He has this thing about ties, which is that he wears them all the time and he plays with them when he's thinking. The one he's wearing today has fat blue stripes and narrow yellow ones. "Is she mean?"

"No."

"A snob?" he asks, flapping harder.

"No."

"Then what?"

"Well," I say, "she's smart."

He stops flapping because he thinks he gets what I'm saying. "Oh, and she rubs it in?"

"Not exactly."

"Then what?"

I scrunch down in the seat and put my knees up on the seat in front of me. Because it's hot out and I'm wearing shorts, it's pretty easy to get my knees to stick there. If the weather isn't just right, they slide off. "I don't know. Yesterday she bumped me in the lunch line. I almost dropped my milk."

Andy shrugs. "Everybody gets bumped in the lunch line."

"She's just always in my way, KWIM?" That is code for "know what I mean."

"Not really," Andy says. "It sounds to me like there's nothing wrong with her."

"That's what's wrong with her," I grumble. "She's perfect."

"Why should you care?" Andy asks.

The only thing about Andy is that sometimes he forgets whose side he's on. "I don't," I say, picking at a scab on my knee. I bet perfect people don't even have scabs to pick, because they never fall down. The truth is that I don't care *much*. And I wouldn't care at all, if only Mr. Mooney would stop sunning his smile on Ellie.

In school we learned about the Sahara Desert and how it gets sunshine all day long, every day. That's about how much sunshine Ellie gets in our class. It wouldn't kill her to share a little.

Haiku #7
By Mary Margaret

Sticky sweet and red
A blob so still, sitting there
Ellie is smelly

I chew on my eraser and read what I wrote. When I get to the last line, I stop. I meant to write *"jelly* is smelly," but I smile at my mistake before I add a *j*, so it's *jellie*. I read it one more time. Mr. Mooney told us haikus are supposed to be about nature, but jelly comes from fruit, and fruit is nature, so I think a haiku about jelly will count.

I like writing poems, and I'm good at it. There's this rhymey one I wrote about belly buttons. When my new baby sister, Liza, was born, there was this thick rope made out of skin that attached her to Mom, kind of like a lasso. My dad cut the rope, but part of it stuck to Liza. After a while, it fell off and left a belly button. So I wrote this poem.

It doesn't matter
If you're a girl or a son
Everybody gets
A belly *but*ton!

The last line sounds best if you shout it, but JT made me stop after a while. He said it was annoying. JT is my brother. He's thirteen and a computer wiz. He runs on a cross-country team, too, which means he runs through fields and woods and stuff. I don't really get why. I mean, there isn't even a ball that they have to chase, like in soccer. They are just running. Anyway, he's a pretty good brother, except that he thinks lots of things are annoying. When the orange juice is all gone, that's annoying. When a Web site takes a long time to come onto the computer screen, that's really annoying. He hates that. And it's annoying when this girl Dana calls him on the phone. The worst thing I can say about anything is that it's stupid. The worst thing JT can say about anything is that it's annoying.

My mom comes in, holding a pen in her teeth. "'Ow's 'ah 'omework?" she asks. She's carrying Baby Liza in one arm and the phone in the other. The calendar she uses to write down all her meetings is kind of trapped between her arm and her body. Turning sideways, she squeezes through the space that's between my chair and the wall. Not very long ago she was so gigantically big that she would have gotten stuck back there, like that time Winnie-the-Pooh got stuck in Rabbit's hole because he'd eaten too much honey. But that's because she was hugely pregnant with Liza. Now she's not, and it's a big relief to me that she's done with all that.

"Good. Listen to this." I read her my haiku.

"'Ice,'" she says. When she smiles, it looks like something hurts because the pen is still in her mouth. Liza starts to cry. My mom jounces her a little bit, but she only cries harder. Even though Liza cries less than she used to, she still cries a lot. My mom and dad and JT have gotten used to it, but not me.

Ever since Liza got here, things have been different. My mom is busier, because when Liza wants something, she wants it right away. That was a lot worse at first than it is now, but it's still hard. Some good stuff has happened. I got Hershey, my rabbit. What I really wanted was a dog, but that hasn't worked out (yet), because my dad is allergic to pet hair. Hershey stays in a hutch outside.

"'Ow did 'oo decide to white abow Ellie?" my mom asks.

"It's not about Ellie," I say. I hear enough about Ellie at school. Do I have to hear about her at home, too? "It's about jelly!"

She nods. "'Ite. I know, 'ut—" Liza has turned her volume way up, and I'm tired of trying to talk loud enough for my mom to hear. I jab my finger toward my ear. "I can't hear you, but never mind," I say. I heap up my homework into my arms and stomp to my room.

The thing is, home used to be a certain way, like we'd always have dinner at 6:00, and then we'd play a board game together. But then Liza came out and changed all that. Mom says Liza doesn't know about our family rules, like no temper tantrums during dinner. But sometimes I catch Liza looking around, sneaky-like. She sees that we're just getting ready to play a game or something—I *know* she sees it—and then she'll burst out crying. It's like she decides to ruin it on purpose. She knows the rules; she just doesn't follow them. I like her more than I did at first, but she's what Mr. Mooney calls "disruptive in class."

So when school started, I was glad. I liked getting away from Liza and going someplace where everyone follows the same rules. In the mornings we do group projects and math. Specials are in the afternoon—art on Monday, gym on Tuesday and Thursday, music on Wednesday—right after SQUIRT (super-quiet ultra-independent reading time). I can count on it. I can also count on the teacher liking me best, because it seems like the teacher always likes me best. At least that's the way it was until *Ellie*.

When I remember that, even stomping up the stairs extra hard and slamming my door doesn't make me feel any better.

Later, when I'm setting knives and spoons on the table (I always do the forks last because they look so mean), the phone rings. Mom is changing Liza's diaper, and JT is upstairs in his room, so I answer it.

"Hello?"

"Hi." It's a girl's voice. "Is JT there?"

"What?" I say, even though I heard her. I just want some time to think.

"Oh! Do I have the wrong number?" she asks. She sounds nervous, and I almost feel sorry for her. Almost. Except that she is a girl. And she is calling my brother.

"No," I say. I twist my ponytail around and around my finger, counting the twists. "This is probably the right number."

"Probably?"

"Well, we do have a JT in our house."

"Can I talk to him?"

I think about this. Girl + phone call = annoying. JT and I get along pretty good most of the time. He helps me with my homework, and he lets me tag along when he goes downtown. I'm only nine, so there's not that much I can do to pay him back. But this is something I can do.

"No," I say. "He's not here."

"But . . . ? I thought you just said there's a JT there."

"We have one in our family, but he's not here right now."

"Oh." She sounds disappointed.

I don't say anything.

"Could you . . ." Then she stops.

"What?" I ask. This talking on the phone with girls is pretty boring. No wonder JT gets annoyed. I look out the window into the backyard.

"Could you . . . take a message?" She asks it the way I ask for a second cookie when I'm pretty sure my mom will say no.

"Okay." My eyes land on Hershey's hut, and suddenly I remember that I haven't fed her yet today.

"Tell him that Kirsty called? And ask him to call me back?"

I'm not really listening because once I start thinking about Hershey, I wonder if I forgot to latch her cage. I think I did, but what if I didn't? What if she got out and is hopping all around the neighborhood? By now a dog might have thought she was his chew toy and chewed her to bits. "Sure," I say. "Bye." I race out to Hershey's shed and fling open the door. Hershey looks up at me and blinks. Then she hops over to her food dish. And I grin a big grin because Hershey knows that I'm the one who feeds her. I'm the one who takes care of her. She loves me.

By the end of that night, it seems like Hershey's the *only* one who does. Mom is mad at me because I never finished setting the table, and she had to do it. When I try to explain about checking on Hershey, she just says, "No excuses, Mary Margaret. I don't ask much of you. I expect that you'll do the things I *do* ask of you."

After dinner, I flop down to read the newspaper. Mr. Mooney makes us read it every night, and we have to talk in class about something we've read. Tomorrow it's my turn, but Mr. Mooney says I have to talk about something that's happened in a different city, not ours. I don't get why we have to know about what's going on in other places. If it's happening someplace else, then why should I care? Too bad I said that to Mr. Mooney, because then he told me that I have to find something that's happening outside of our town *and* tell why I should care about it.

"What're you doing?" JT asks, looking over my shoulder. I tell him.

He sits down on the arm of the chair. "What've you got so far?"

"A two-headed cow was born in Houston."

JT shakes his head.

"Well, here's one about a movie star who—"

"Here!" JT says. He points at an article that's about someone who wants to be governor. "This one is perfect."

"Boring," I say.

"Not hardly. Governors sign bills into law. The governor is the reason that you have to put your seat belt on when you ride in the car."

"I use the seat belt because it's stupid not to—not because somebody tells me to," I say. But I know JT is right. Mr. Mooney will like a current event about a governor. I get the scissors and cut the article out.

Before I put the newspaper away, I look again at the story I started to tell JT about. There's a picture of a movie star named Caleb Strong taking a bite of a big hunk of raw broccoli. The story says that the celebrities are posing with their favorite fruit or vegetable to raise money for the cancer society. I feel sad that I won't be using that story. The kids in my class go wild over actors, no matter what they are eating.

I fold the newspaper up and put it back on the coffee table so my dad will be able to find it. He gets really crabby when he can't find it, and he's the kind of guy who doesn't get crabby that often. In fact, he's a pretty fun guy, at least for a grown-up. Since Liza was born, him and me have been doing more things together. He's subbing for Mom for a while, just like another teacher subs for Mr. Mooney when he's sick.

"I'm ready for someone to put me to bed," I say. "Who's the lucky winner tonight?"

"Me, me, me!" shouts my dad, racing up the stairway. That's the thing about my dad. He really does get that excited over things like tucking me in. We settle down together on my bed, and after he reads me some of my book, he says, "How was your day?"

"It was okay."

"Tell me one good thing and one bad thing."

I roll onto my stomach so I can see him better. This is one of my favorite parts of the day, when it's just me and him. I guess you could say that he adores me. "The good thing was that Dante got trapped in the teachers' bathroom at school."

"That's the *good* thing?"

"Well, yeah! Because it was exciting. He got in there and locked the door, but somehow the door broke. And he's very fidgety and nervous even when he's not trapped in a bathroom. One of the teachers thought he was going to pass on in there."

"You mean pass out?"

"Yeah, pass out. So the teachers tried to distract him. One started asking him math questions through the door, like 'What's four times eighty?' but that made him more nervous because he's bad at math, and he doesn't get that trick about just adding a zero. He sounded like he was going to cry. Then Drew said we should ask him about soccer, because he loves soccer, and he can tell you who won which match and by how much for like the last twenty years!"

"Did that work?"

"Better than the math did. And we had it all worked out how we were going to slide food in to him under the door so he wouldn't starve. We took turns talking to him through the door while the teachers tried to figure out how to get him out."

"And did they?"

I nod. "You know Mrs. Capotosto? Our janitor? She finally just unscrewed the door from the wall. But he was stuck in there for a pretty long time."

"If that was the good thing," he says, "I'm not sure I want to hear the bad thing."

I'm not sure I even want to think about the bad thing. I lay my head down on my pillow, close my eyes, and yawn a very big yawn. "I'm too sleepy," I say.

He pokes me in my side. "Come on. You're not getting off that easy. What was the bad thing?"

So then I tell him all about that stupid test Mr. Mooney gave us on following directions. After I'm done telling him all that, I groan.

"Well," he says, rolling out of my bed, "I know it wasn't fun, but it sounds like it was a good test."

"What do you mean? It was an awful test! And it wasn't even fair!"

"But you learned something, maybe. And that would make it a good thing, right?"

I hate it when he tries to make my bad thing into a good thing, so I don't say anything.

"No prayer poem tonight?" he asks.

I shake my head.

He shuts off the light. "All right, then. You'll feel better about it tomorrow," he says, "after a good night of sleep."

My dad thinks a good night of sleep takes care of everything. Maybe it would have, too, if my dad hadn't gone back downstairs and tried to read the paper. But he did, and then he yelled at me from the bottom of the stairs, "Mary MARGARET! How many TIMES have I TOLD you NOT to cut something OUT of the paper until I'm DONE reading it?" He didn't even notice that I had put the paper and the scissors back where they belonged.

Getting yelled at by a person who adores you is not the greatest way to end a day. Especially when the day already stinks high to the sky. It's hard to get to sleep after that. But it works out good for JT that I get yelled at, because if Dad hadn't yelled at me, then I would have fallen asleep right away. And I wouldn't have remembered about the girl who called. But since I got yelled at and couldn't fall asleep, that gives me time to remember.

I climb out of bed and go to JT's room. He's got his headphones on. He always listens to music while he does his homework. I pull one side of the headphones away from his head. "JT," I say, "some girl called you today."

He pulls his headphones off. "Where was I? I've been home ever since school got out."

"In your room. I thought I'd get rid of her for you."

"Oh, it was Dana?"

"No."

"Then who was it?"

That's a good question, I think. What was her name again? "I don't know," I say.

"Well, think!" he says, all bossy. "It's kind of important."

"Christy or Kersten . . . I don't remember exactly because when she said it, I was thinking about Hershey and . . ." The frown on his face makes me stop for a second, then I say, "Maybe it was Kirsty?"

"Maybe? Oh, that's great. Just great." But the way he says it makes me mad. He doesn't think it's great at all.

"I was just helping you! You said that girls who call on the phone are annoying."

"No, I said that *Dana* is annoying. Why don't you listen?"

"I do listen!" I say. And then, because I'm mad at him, I touch a few things on his desk. I start small. I roll a pencil across his deck, then play with a couple of magnets. He is looking at me like he's going to kill me. But I know that he won't, so I move a stack of books until they are hanging halfway off his desk. If I shove them over just a little farther, they'll tip and fall.

"Stop it, capiche?" he says. "Capiche" is just JT's fancy way of saying "Know what I mean?" I might capiche, but that doesn't mean I stop. I pick up a CD and press my fingers right on it. Then I hold it up to the light and flick it back and forth so I can see my fingerprints.

That does it. JT flies up out of his chair and butts me like Billy Goat Gruff out of his room. "You. Are. So. *Annoying!*" he yells. Then he slams the door.

Annoying? Annoying? I can't believe that JT has called me the worst thing he can think of when all I did was help him out. "Oh, yeah?" I yell at the door. "Well, you're . . . you're stupid!"

When I come down for breakfast the next morning, my mom hasn't had her coffee yet. That means that she is still mostly asleep even though her eyes are open. My dad and JT are already gone. It feels like everyone is still mad at me at home.

At school, Brett, Kyle, and McKenzie are definitely still mad at me. That's because Harry, who is in perfect Ellie's group, is teasing us about yesterday's test. "What igits!" he says while the class is lining up for lunch. "I can't believe you actually sang all the way to the office—if you can call that squawking noise singing."

McKenzie sticks her chin out. "It's not my fault," she says. "I tried to tell her, but she always has to do things her way."

Before I can think of something zippy to say that will make Harry be quiet, Mr. Mooney asks me to help him get some things from the supply closet. Normally I would be happy about that. Teachers usually only ask their favorite students to help them. But Mr. Mooney wants to talk about that test, too.

"What did you think of that test?" He unlocks the supply closet.

I shrug.

He laughs a little. "Don't tell me you don't have an opinion," he says. "I know you, and you have an opinion about everything. Let me have it. What did you think of the test?" He drops a big stack of yellow construction paper into my arms, which I'm holding out like a forklift.

"Uhhh!" I grunt. "Not much."

He throws on another stack. Black this time. Yellow paper + black paper = bumblebees? "You didn't like it."

"It was a trick test."

"Why do you think that?"

"Because this test didn't have answers. You made us think it had answers, but it didn't. It wasn't fair."

"Mary Margaret, the very first instruction was to read all the instructions. I believe I even said that as I was handing out the test."

"But tests are supposed to have answers!" I say, louder than I mean to.

"The answer was to stop taking the test," Mr. Mooney says.

"It wasn't just me. There were lots of groups that did all that stuff on the test," I say.

"We're not talking about them," he says. "We're talking about you. You let your group down because of what you wanted—to be first."

I can't believe this! First my dad and JT are mad at me,

and now it feels like Mr. Mooney is yelling at me, even though he's still using a quiet voice. I want to clap my hands over my ears so that I don't have to hear any more, but my arms are full, so there's nothing I can do except listen when he says, "You're very independent and creative, but working cooperatively isn't easy for you. You could learn a few things from Ellie." When he says that, I want to bolt away fast like Hershey does when a loud noise surprises her. But I am all weighed down with construction paper, like an anchor, and I have to just stand there.

Mr. Mooney squats down and pushes a bucket of used crayons out of the way so he can get to the new boxes of markers. Suddenly I feel like I'm that bucket of dull, stubby crayons, all melted and waxy, and Ellie is the new marker, all smooth and cool. The kind that makes sharp, bright lines. The kind, I think, scuffing down the hall behind Mr. Mooney back to the classroom, that everyone loves.

By the time I get to lunch, the only seat that's left in the cafeteria is one at the very end of the table. Ellie is sitting catty-corner from me. I unwrap my sandwich—peanut butter and jelly and cheese. It's a new recipe I thought up. Yesterday I had a banana and mayo sandwich—another of my specialties. My mom says I can make any kind of sandwich I want as long as it's healthy and I eat what I make.

My lunches are interesting, but they don't always work out that good. I look down at my sandwich and see that the cheese is sliding out of the sandwich. A few seats away,

Noah and Kyle are fighting over whose turn it is to spin a dime, and McKenzie is sucking her applesauce up through a straw. Brittney takes a spoonful of yogurt and spits little white drops everywhere when she says, "Ellie, I'll trade you my chips for your pear."

Ellie must be the only kid in the world who actually finishes chewing her food and swallows before talking, just like grown-ups want us to. "I would, except my mom doesn't want me to trade my lunch food," she says. "I'm sorry!" And she sounds like she really is sorry, too. I watch her as she just sits there and eats. Nothing is falling out of her sandwich. But I bet it's really boring.

When I'm coming in from recess, I see Ellie standing by the bulletin board outside the office. She's reading a poster so hard that she doesn't even hear McKenzie say "Hi" to her. I know she doesn't because Ellie always says "Hi" back to everyone who says "Hi" to her. Always. This makes me wonder what she is reading. I stop beside her. "What are you reading?" I ask.

When she looks at me, her eyes are sparkly. "It's about auditions for a play—*Cinderella*! I think I'd like to be in it, but I don't know if I'd be very good."

I know it's not polite to say "You're right." And I don't want to say "Sure, you'd be good." First, I don't know if she'd be good or not, and two, like I said, she already gets enough sunshine, and she'll only get more if she's in this play. So I just say, "Hmmm."

Then I read the poster myself. It says it is a community play, but the entire cast and crew will be kids under the age of fourteen. At the bottom of the poster, it says, "For more information, contact Mr. Mooney, Director." And that reminds me about how Mr. Mooney is not very excited about me right now. He's more excited about . . . I look at Ellie out of the corner of my eye . . . *her*. I think of how Ellie can do everything better than me—even follow directions—and how she's always quiet when she's supposed to be. And then I remember that she's quiet even when she doesn't have to be. She's kind of shy. I feel a happy ping inside of me. Quiet Ellie up onstage? In front of all those people? *Her?*

And suddenly I know absolutely positively with sugar on top that I've found the thing that I'll be better at than Ellie. I've found the thing that will make Mr. Mooney like me better than he likes her. I will be the star of his play. I will be *Cinderella!* In my mind, I can already see myself onstage taking a bow. I can hear everyone clapping for me, me, me! My mom and dad and JT are all in the audience (not Liza, though, because she'd cry and spoil it), clapping. Best of all, Mr. Mooney is backstage, beaming a big smile at me so bright it's like a spotlight, lighting me up onstage.

I walk to our classroom and sit down in my chair, thinking about how it's going to be so perfect. The only thing I need is a more glamorous name. My name is okay. It's just a little boring, like having buttered toast for breakfast every morning. The toast isn't bad, but it could do with some zip. My name could do with some zip, too. Mary the Magnificent? That sounds like I'm a magician. Mary Marvelous? Too braggy. I want something that sounds like I'm special. Mary Margar . . . *eeeet*. *Eeeet*. Next to me, Kyle is pulling his chair out, and it is scraping across the floor.

And that is how I come up with my famous name—Mary *Marguerite*. I practice saying it a few times different ways and discover that it sounds best when the *eet* part comes out like a sigh. Mary Marguer-*ite*. It's special. It's glamorous. It's me.

Andy has his violin lesson after school, so he's not on the bus. I am about ready to pop if I don't tell someone that I'm going to be in the play. "Hey, Stevie Butts," I say, twisting around in my seat. "I'm going to be Cinderella."

He leans over the seat. "For Halloween?"

"No, in a play."

"Neat." He is looking at my lunch box, so I dig out a cookie and give it to him. "Thanks, Mary Margaret." He chomps a big bite off and then gets a funny look on his face. "What kind of cookie is *this*?"

"Oh, oatmeal mustard. I thought I might like cookies if they were, you know, different. So I made up my own. I forgot all about that." He gives me the rest of the cookie back, and I try it. "Hmm. There's too much of something in here," I say.

"Mustard?"

I shake my head. "I'll figure it out. My next batch will be better." I look out the window for the rest of the bus ride and daydream about being a star.

When I get home, there's a note on the counter.

Liza's napping. I'm on a work call. Snack in fridge.
                                                    —Mom

I take my snack—a cut-up apple—to the table and munch it down while I think about my day. I wait until I think Andy will be home from his lesson and then pick up the phone to call him and tell him all about the play. My mom plans parties—big ones for big companies—and she works from home. That's why we have two phone lines. Line one is for home calls. Line two is for work calls. I carefully push the line one button before I pick up the phone, but I pick it up quietly, just in case I'm on line two by mistake.

As soon as I put the phone to my ear, a girl's voice says, ". . . at the mall."

For a minute I'm confused. Is this my mom's work call? Sometimes she has to order cakes, and there's a cake store at the mall. But I'm sure I pressed line one. In the middle of being confused, I hear JT laugh. Then I get it! He's on the home line but upstairs. Before I can hang up, the girl giggles—"Tee-hee-hee!"—like a . . . like a girl who is boy crazy.

And then I do a bad thing. I snort. I can't help it! JT on the phone with a girl who tee-hee-hees?

"Mary Margaret?" JT says. I gasp and slam the phone down. "MARY MARGARET!" he yells, and I can hear him all the way from upstairs. But I don't answer. That works for about two minutes, until he marches into the kitchen.

"What do you think you're doing?"

"Homework," I say. I bend over my book and frown all serious so that maybe he'll believe me.

"I heard you. You were eavesdropping."

"Was not." But then "Tee-hee-hee" comes out of my mouth, too.

JT's face gets pink. Then it turns the color of tomato soup. By the time it's as red as a rotten tomato, Mom has come down from her office. Which makes me very relieved. Until I see that she's almost as mad as JT.

"JT, why were you yelling up there? Didn't I tell you I was going to be on a call?"

"Mary Margaret was listening in on my private phone call!"

"Was not!" I say. "I just picked up the phone to call Andy. Why would I want to listen to you talk to some girl?" I make a face. Then I giggle again. I think I'm getting pretty good at tee-hee-hee-ing. JT doesn't think so.

"She was, too, Mom! She was eavesdropping. And last night she was touching everything on my desk." Then he does something that I never thought he'd do. He tattles. "And she called me stupid!"

My mother points her finger at me like it's a magic

wand, and she says the *G* word. "Grounded," she says. "Three days."

"That's not fair! He called me annoying!" I shoot back.

"That's no excuse. Calling anyone stupid is unacceptable." *Unacceptable* is my mother's new favorite word, it seems like. Her old favorite word was *exhausted*. She used it a lot when she was pregnant and right after Liza was born. Right now I think I like her old favorite word better. Too bad she's not done talking at me yet. "It's demeaning," she says. "It's okay to call things stupid—like when Dad calls the DVD player stupid—but not people."

"Then why can JT call me annoying?"

"Because that describes the way someone is acting—not their intelligence. Big difference," she says.

Then I remember something. Anyone who wants to be in the play has to be at a meeting on Saturday morning. HAS to. No exceptions. That's what Mr. Mooney said when I asked him about it. And Saturday is only two days away. "But you can't ground me!" I say. And then I explain everything about the play and about how I have to be at the meeting.

"Please, Mama," I say. Mama is what I call her when something is really important to me. "Please?"

"I'm sorry. You know the rules. No exceptions for grounding." Then she leaves.

I scowl at JT, who hasn't tattled on me since the time I tried to sneak Dad's smiley-face underwear to school for

Show and Tell. He scowls right back at me, but his scowl is meaner. He's thirteen, so he's had more practice. I guess you could say we're in each other's doghouse. Which is not the best place to be when usually you like your brother. Or when you need him to help you get what you want.

How long are you going to be mad?" JT asks. It's Saturday morning, and I'm watching cartoons. I didn't say anything to him all day yesterday. Not one word. Which is harder than it looks when you're me.

"That depends," I say. On TV that dumb Wile E. Coyote has run off a cliff again. Road Runner is flicking his tongue out at him.

"On what?"

I watch the coyote crash down to the bottom of the canyon and get squashed flat by a truck. "On how long you live," I say.

That cracks JT up. He busts out laughing. I try not to, but then I start laughing, too, because it was pretty funny. After we laugh together like that, I can't make myself be mad at him, even though I want to.

He knows right away that I can't be mad anymore. "I'm sorry I ratted on you," he says. "I didn't know that Mom would get all extreme."

"Grounded for"—I pound the arm of the chair three times—"three whole days!"

"I think she got carried away because she was mad at both of us. It stinks that you'll miss the meeting about the play."

I look up at the clock. "I haven't missed it yet," I say. "I bet you could think of a way to change her mind if you wanted to."

"I'm not *that* smart," he says. Now Foghorn Leghorn— the big rooster—is on, and we watch it together. Foghorn Leghorn is trying to protect a little chick from a dog, so he hammers up a sign that says "No Dogs Allowed." The dog says, "I'm no dog. I'm a hound." And then Foghorn says, "I say! That is a tech-ni-cal-i-ty! You hear me, boy?"

"What's a technicality?" I ask.

JT doesn't answer right away. He stares at the TV, and then his lips twitch into a smile. "It's what's going to change Mom's mind," he says.

I follow him into the kitchen, where Mom is giving Liza a bath in the sink. To me, Liza looks like a big vegetable that never got ripe. "Mom," he says. "I think you should ease up on Mary Motormouth and let her go to that meeting this morning." JT always plays around with my name. That's how he lets me know he likes me—except for when it bugs me.

"You know how I feel about calling people stupid," she says.

"Yeah, I know," JT says. "But I've been thinking, and Mary Margaret didn't call me stupid."

I didn't? I think. But I'm smart enough not to say that out loud.

"She didn't?" my mom says.

"Not technically. When we were fighting, I closed the door, and *then* she said 'You're stupid,' so she actually called the door stupid." My mom raises an eyebrow at JT. "Seriously," he says. "I feel bad I got her in so much trouble when all she did was call the door stupid. I'll walk her down to the meeting if you'll lift the embargo."

My mother starts to shake her head, but before she can say anything, JT offers to take Liza along in the stroller. "That way you can have a nice cup of coffee by yourself—and a shower," he says. Then he elbows me when she's not looking, and suddenly I know what he wants me to do.

"And I won't call anyone stupid, Mom—ever. I promise."

"All right," she says, looking from me to JT. She says it like she's not sure it's all right.

"All *right!*" I say, and I run out of there quick before she can change her mind.

I slide into a chair in the back row just as Mr. Mooney is getting up onstage to start the meeting. JT has to wait around for me so he can walk me home, so he rolls the stroller in right behind me. Liza fell asleep on the walk, so that's good. Maybe for once she'll keep her mouth shut.

I look around. Most of the kids are there with one of their parents. Ellie is in the front row with a lady who's probably her mom. It's easy to see where Ellie gets all that perfectness. When her mom turns to pat down Ellie's hair, I can see that she's wearing pink nail polish. She has a pink sweater on, and she's carrying a pink purse. All the pinks match. Ellie is wearing a skirt—on a Saturday! I look down at my stretchy pants and my V-neck shirt that I'm wearing backwards—I like the V in the back—and I wonder if we're going to be graded on what we're wearing. If we are, I feel kind of sorry for Ellie.

Mr. Mooney explains the meeting was supposed to be about stuff like auditions and practices. "But," he says, "a more pressing issue has come up—to wit, there are not enough funds to mount the production. Unless we figure out a way to raise enough money, we won't be able to put on the play."

Everyone groans like they have stomachaches. Mr. Mooney holds up his hand. "Think of it as a challenge," he says. "An opportunity to exercise our brains." He picks up a marker and says, "Let's brainstorm some ideas."

We—the grown-ups, actually—spend a long time talking about ideas. Bake sale? Car wash? Mr. Mooney writes every idea down on a big sheet of paper. Every time a grown-up says something, I slink farther down in my seat. The only reason the grown-ups even got to come to our meeting was to give their kids rides, and now they are taking over. When some man in a tie says, "How about a corporate sponsorship?" I can't keep my mouth to myself anymore. I pop my hand up.

"Yes?" Mr. Mooney says.

"I thought the kids were going to do everything for this play," I say. "I have the paper about it right here, and it says . . ." I hold up the paper and read exactly what it says. "'This is a community play put on entirely by kids.'"

"That's right," he says. He doesn't get what I'm saying.

"But the *parents* are doing this part," I say. I wave my hand at the man in the tie. "That corporate thingy—whatever he said—I don't even know what it is."

Mr. Mooney snaps his fingers. "You're absolutely right!" he says. "Thank you, Mary Margaret, for pointing that out." When he says that, it feels like fireworks go off inside me. My plan to get Mr. Mooney to like me again is already working. Then he says, "Thespians, what thinkest thou?"

"Huh?" I say.

But Ellie knows what he's talking about. "Maybe we raise money by doing odd jobs for people."

"Good idea, Ellie," Mr. Mooney says. He writes it down on a big sheet of paper.

Humph! I think. I can do better than that. I wave my hand in the air again to get Mr. Mooney to look at me instead of at that Ellie. "Mr. Mooney! Mr. Mooney!"

"What's your idea, Mary Margaret?"

I yank my hand out of the air. I don't actually have an idea quite yet. "I forgot," I say.

"Let's sell our old clothes," says a girl.

"No! Let's have a used pet sale!" shouts a boy. I think he must be nuts. Who would want to sell their pet?

"Couldn't we just ask the President for money?" asks his little brother.

"Don't be dumb," the pet boy says. "The President doesn't just give money to anyone."

At the same time he says that, another kid says, "My school sold wrapping paper and calendars one year. How about that?"

I clap my hands over my ears because it's so noisy I can't think. I don't hear what the girl in front of me says, but I see her hop up and hold up her thumb to her mouth like it's a microphone. She looks like she's pretending to be a rock star.

That makes me think about the picture of the celebrity I saw in the paper—the one who was eating broccoli. And that's when I get the great idea. Calendars + celebrities + pets = money = we get to put on the play = I get to be Cinderella!

I leap out of my seat like someone has jabbed me with a pin. "We can do a calendar!" I shout.

"Hey, I already said that," says the boy whose school sold stuff to raise money.

"Not just boring calendars," I say. I'm trying to talk as fast as my brain is telling me stuff. "Calendars that we put together—calendars of celebrities and their pets. Everyone would want to buy one."

Harry, the only other kid besides Ellie that I recognize, says, "No celebrity is going to agree to be in our dinky calendar, Mary Margaret. They don't care about our play. Not unless we pay them a lot of money. You think they do that stuff for free?"

I hadn't thought of that. "Well, they *might*," I shoot back.

"Not a chance."

Mr. Mooney writes down my idea, then asks, "What else?"

Someone says something else, but I'm not listening anymore. I'm harrump-ing because they didn't like my idea. JT leans over to me and says, "It's a good idea, but a little half-baked."

"What's that supposed to mean?"

"That it could work, but you need to think about it a little more. Maybe you don't need celebrities. What's so great about celebrities, anyway?"

I think JT is playing dumb. "They're famous."

"Which means?"

"That everybody in the world knows *who they are*."

"Yeah, but you wouldn't be selling to everybody in the world. You'd just be selling to people around here." Liza wakes up and—big surprise—she starts to cry. JT stands up. "I'm going to take her out in the hall," he says.

"But what about my idea?"

He raps his knuckles on my head. "It needs another minute in the oven. You'll figure it out. I'll be back in a while." Then he rolls Liza out.

I think fast. It's a good idea. I know it is! It would work because people like pets, and everyone needs a calendar. But you can buy a pet calendar anywhere. The famous people is what would make it special. JT is right that we wouldn't need to sell it to everyone in the world. Just to people around here. I think about how I might sell the calendars. I could tell Mr. Gibbons about them. He's our crossing guard. I sit there thinking about Mr. Gibbons, who is about as old as Moses and has been the crossing guard at our school forever. Mr. Gibbons knows all the kids, and all their parents, and even some of their grandparents. It seems like Mr. Gibbons knows everyone . . . *and*, I think, *and EVERYONE in town knows Mr. Gibbons!*

I pop up out of my seat again. "Mr. Mooney! Mr. Mooney!" And when he says, "Yes, Mary Margaret," I tell everyone the whole thing—how we'll get people from around our town to pose with their pets. We'll get people who are famous to nobody but us.

When I'm done explaining, the man in the tie says, "But isn't it expensive to get calendars made?"

"JT made one for my grandparents for Christmas once," I say. "He took pictures with his digital camera and then set the whole thing up on his computer."

"We'd still have to pay for printing," says Mr. Mooney. "But I think it might work. What does everyone think? Is this an idea worth pursuing?"

Suddenly everyone is talking at the same time again, only this time I don't want to cover my ears because they are all talking about who to put on the calendar—which was my idea. So in a way they are all talking about me! When JT comes back in with Liza, I say to everyone, "Hey, this is JT. He's the one who is going to make the calendars so we can put on the play!" All the kids start clapping, and the grown-ups are all smiling at him, and I'm so happy that I'm going to get to be Cinderella—maybe, probably—that I give him a monster hug, right there in front of everybody. But I guess I embarrass JT, because all he can do is stand there like a flagpole wearing sneakers.

"Right, JT?" I say, hugging him harder. I know the "yes" must be stuck in JT's throat, and if I squeeze him hard enough, it will come out. "Right?"

Everyone is staring at him, all hopeful and happy. He looks at me and then at them, and then he says, "Ah, excuse us for a second." Then he pushes the stroller with one hand, and he grabs me with the other and pulls me out into the hall, but not before I yell over my shoulder, "He's just a little shy."

When the door closes behind us, he hisses, "I am *not* shy. I'm mad! What did you get me into this time, Mary Maniac?"

"I did what you said. I baked the rest of the idea!" I say. "We can use people from around here and their pets. And I told them that you would make the calendar, because you did that one for Grandpa and Grandma on the computer, remember? And they loved it! So I figured you could make this one, too." My voice is bright because

I am happy, but I am doing that thing I do when I get nervous, which is talk very fast.

"Did you ever think about how maybe I have a life, too, Mary Margaret? I have cross-country practice and meets, and schoolwork, and Kir—never mind. I'm too busy to run around town taking pictures of everyone and to make the calendar. Get someone else to do it."

"But I already told everyone in there that you would!"

"Then go back in and tell them that I won't!"

"But, JT—"

"No! I convinced Mom to un-ground you so you could come to this thing, and I even brought you down here, but that's as much help as you're going to get from me."

"You could find time if you really wanted to!"

"You're right. But I don't want to! So go back in there and tell them that."

I sigh and scuffle toward the auditorium. But I scuffle very slowly, giving JT time to feel sorry for me and change his mind. I think I hear something, so I stop and turn around, "What?" I say.

"I didn't say anything," he says.

"Oh, I thought you said something. I thought you said, 'Wait. I'll do it.'"

"Nice try," he says. "That would pretty much take a miracle."

I turn around slow and scuffle a few more steps. A miracle *could* happen, if I give it enough time. I read about this dog once that found its way home even though home was 3,000 miles away. So miracles do happen, sometimes. I feel like I'm walking the plank on a pirate ship. Telling everyone that JT won't do my great idea will be like falling into the icy deep darkness of the ocean.

Just as I push the auditorium door open, the miracle happens. A girl comes in the front door. She has long, wavy hair and big brown eyes. When she smiles at JT, she gets little dents in her cheeks. "I'm here for the meeting about the play. Are you going to be in it?"

"Uh, not exactly in it," says JT. But then he adds, "But I'm helping out with raising money for it."

I am so surprised that words pop right out of my mouth. "But you just said—"

"Oh, that," he says. "I was teasing you. You know how I love to tease you." And he comes over and tugs on my ponytail, like we are all of a sudden best friends and not in the middle of him being mad at me.

"Oh, good. I'm Claire, and I want to work backstage," says the girl. She's carrying a purse with fringes and a little book that has a crossword puzzle on the cover. "I hope I'm not too late."

I grab her empty hand and pump it up and down. "I'm Mary Margaret," I say. "And you're just in time."

5. Pet Broccoli?

After we've decided which town celebrities we want to have on our calendar, Mr. Mooney asks for volunteers. Over the next few days, the volunteers are each supposed to talk to one celebrity, explain our (*my*) idea for the Community Calendar. If the person wants to have their picture in our calendar, then we're supposed to also find out what kind of pet they have.

On Tuesday after school we have another big meeting. I write down what everyone found out.

Mr. Gibbons, the crossing guard, has a dog. We all already know Barney. He comes to work with Mr. Gibbons every day. When it rains, they even wear matching yellow slickers.

The mayor has a parrot that talks. "But all he says is 'Promises, promises!'" says Dylan, the boy who talked to the mayor.

Mrs. Stella, who works at the candy store, has a dog.

Vrani has a dog, too. Vrani is a lifeguard at the community pool. She shaved her head once, and she wears

shorts, even in the winter. "I thought she'd have a taran-
tula or something," I say to Rachel, the girl who talked to
Vrani.

"Nope," Rachel says. "It's a white poodle named
Toodles."

"What about Lenny?" I ask. Lenny is an old man who
sits on the bench in front of the post office on nice days and
plays checkers with anyone who wants to play, even kids.

"Pet rock," says a girl named Kate. "I told him about
how we wanted him to be in the calendar. When I asked
him what kind of pet he had, he reached down, picked up
a rock, and then drew a face on it. 'Meet Rocky,' he said.
'I just got him!' Do you think that counts?"

I shrug. "Yeah, sure." I know what it's like not to have
a real pet. My mom got me an ant farm once. I pretended
I was happy about it for a while, but they were a big dis-
appointment. Still, at least they moved around. A pet rock
is only going to sit there. I feel sorry for Lenny.

Miss Davis, the children's librarian, has a snake. "A
snake?" I say to the girl who talked to Miss Davis. "What
kind?"

"The slithery kind," says the girl. "And you know what
else? She feeds it *live* crickets."

Mr. Mooney looks up from the computer, where he's
researching how much it will cost to make the calendar.
"Miss Davis?" he asks. "*Miss Davis?* I guess you don't
really know someone until you know what kind of pet
she has."

By the time I've talked to everyone, we have six dogs, two cats, a parrot, a snake, a pet rock, and their famous-to-us owners for the calendar. "Okay," I say, counting them all up. "That's . . . wait a minute. That's only eleven. We need twelve—one for every month of the year."

"I struck out," says a kid in the back. "Santa didn't want his picture taken." Santa isn't really *Santa*; it's just what we call the man who decorates the park with lights every Christmas and who turns them on each year.

"Why not?" someone else asks.

"He says he's all pictured out," says the first kid. "He says his picture is in the paper every year, and people are tired of looking at him."

I take my clipboard over to Mr. Mooney. "We only have eleven," I say, "but I have an idea for the last one. It might take a few days to see if it will work, though."

Mr. Mooney shakes his head like he feels bad for me. "I'm sure it's a good idea, but we don't have the time to wait," he says. "We have to sell the calendars before we know whether the show can go on, and if we can't tell people exactly who will be in the calendar, they won't buy it."

Everyone else brainstorms some more ideas for who can be on the calendar, but my own idea is so big that it's taking up all the space in my brain. I just sit there and daydream about how great it would be if my idea worked. I'm still daydreaming when Mr. Mooney pulls out a big box and opens it. "I'm not positive yet, but let's assume we'll be able to raise enough money by selling calendars," he says, handing everyone their script for the play. "Auditions are on Thursday."

Thursday! All of us start talking at the same time, which sounds like a bunch of bees buzzing. We sound like one happy beehive.

"Thespians, lend me your ears!" says Mr. Mooney.

"No, thanks," I say. "I need both of mine."

"It's a figure of speech," he says. "It means 'listen.'"

"Oh," I say. He never talks this way during school. It must be director talk. I bet he can't help it, just like Mom can't help it when she talks baby talk to Liza. She'll say things like, "Does Lovey Lou want her ba-ba or her bink-bink?" *Blecch!* Like I said, she can't help it. The good news is she doesn't talk to me that way.

Mr. Mooney says, "When you audition, I'll be checking for several things." He holds up one finger. "First, voice projection. Is your voice is loud enough for the audience to hear you? Can you enunciate the words so the audience understands what you're saying?"

Yes, I think. I'm a loud talker. I look over at Ellie. She's not doing much, just listening and frowning a little. She looks a teeny bit worried.

Mr. Mooney flicks up another finger. "Second, can you follow directions?"

Yes, I think. I can definitely follow directions. Most of the time. When I concentrate very hard.

Finger number three pops up on Mr. Mooney. "Third—and this is a big one—is acting in your heart? Is the character in your heart? Do you feel what your character is feeling?"

Oh, yes! I think. Yes, it is! I'm positive that acting is in my heart! I want to be Cinderella so badly that acting *must* be in my heart, and I can't wait until Thursday to prove it.

I can't get to sleep that night. Partly it's because I'm so excited. But mostly it's because the idea in my head that Mr. Mooney wouldn't listen to needs to get out. Finally, I climb out of bed, turn on the light, and find a pencil and some paper.

Dear Mr. Caleb Strong,

I tap my pencil on the desk very fast. I wonder if you talk to movie stars the same way you talk to average people. I can't think of any other way to talk, though, so I just talk to him normal.

My name is Mary Margaret Anderson. I am nine years old. On Thursday I'm going to try out for my very first play. The Sunnydale Stage Door Players are putting on *Cinderella!* I'm going to be Cinderella, probably, because I am very dramatic. Everyone says so. Another reason I am going to win that part is that we need to raise some money, and I thought of the idea of how to do that. We're making a calendar of famous (to us) people and their pets. Then we are going to sell the calendar. We need one more person to be in it. Harry (he's a boy in my class who sits kind of close to me but actually closer to Kyle) says a big celebrity like you would never want to be in our calendar. But I think you might. One, Harry is wrong a lot. Two, I think you remember what it was like before you got richer than the President of the United States. I bet you remember how much fun it was when you were in your first play, before you had to do it for a job. I remember how much fun it used to be when I learned to read. It's still fun, but now I have to do it for school, so it's not the same. I bet acting is a little bit that way for you now.

The number three reason is that I saw the picture of you posing with a piece of broccoli, so you probably won't mind posing with your pet. If you don't have a real pet, maybe you could draw some eyes onto the broccoli and say it's a pet broccoli. Like a pet rock, only use a vegetable instead of a rock. I bet you would make pet vegetables very popular!

Your friend,

Mary Margaret

P.S. As an extra bonus, free of charge, I will send you a #2 Tote if you send me your address. It's for carrying doggy do-do. Maybe you already have a servant that does that for you, but in case you don't.

After I finish that letter, I think about how I'll be famous someday. I think about how anybody could be famous. Maybe even Mr. Daria, that guy who wants to be governor, will be famous. You just never know. And so I write him a letter, too.

Dear Mr. Daria. I remember about how Harry laughed at my current event when I said Mr. Daria's name. "Sounds like diarrhea," he said. And then everyone started laughing at my current event. But at least then it wasn't boring. We need to raise some money to put on a play, so we are making a calendar of people who are famous to us. We probably already have enough people, and you're not even famous, but just in case, could you send me a picture of you with your pet? Thanks a lot.

Your friend,

Mary Margaret

I feel better now that I have gotten my idea out of my head. Mr. Mooney said it would take too long to hear back from Caleb Strong. It would if I sent the letter through the mail, but maybe I could just call him. I wander into JT's room. "JT, will you help me look up the number for Caleb Strong?"

"The actor? His number is probably unlisted. If his number was in the book, everyone would be calling him all the time."

I hold up the letters I wrote. "I really want to ask him about being on the calendar."

"You're still stuck on that idea?"

"I'm not stuck on it. It's stuck on me, KWIM?"

"No, I don't know what you mean. It's a waste of time."

"I just want to try. It's not going to hurt anyone if I try, right?"

"Okay, okay!" He puts both hands up. "I guess we could try to find an e-mail address."

JT is an expert on the computer. After a few minutes, he finds what he's looking for. He points to the screen. "Look. It's an e-mail address at his movie studio," he says. "If we're lucky, the studio will send it to him." He types my letter into the computer and sends it. Then he does the one for the man who wants to be governor, too. His e-mail address is easier to find.

Just as we're sending it, my dad comes in. "Aren't you up a little late?" he asks me.

"I couldn't sleep," I say. "It was too crowded in my head. But I think I'll be able to now."

"It was another idea for the calendar," JT says to Dad.

"Will you be able to raise enough money just from the calendar?"

"Mr. Mooney thinks so." Then I tell him that as soon as we know who is going to be on the calendar, we're going to start selling them. People will have to pay ahead of time because we need the money right now to buy the costumes and sets and stuff like that.

I remember the time that my neighbor Jolene said she'd sell me her Love-Me, Squeeze-Me, Hold-Me Puppy for a dollar. Those things cost about thirty dollars in the store, so I said okay and gave her my dollar. She said she had to go in the house to get it, but she never came out, and then it was time for bed. The next day I asked her about it, but she said she didn't know what I was talking about. Jolene can be that way sometimes. She's five and spoiled. "I wouldn't hand over money without getting something right away," I say as my dad walks me back to my bed.

"Grown-ups do it all the time," he says.

Maybe grown-ups shouldn't be the ones running the world, I think as I snuggle down in my bed. Because it seems to me like they just aren't as smart as they pretend to be.

6. Cinder Ellie

Kind sir," I yell, "would you like to dance?" It's Thursday afternoon during auditions. I'm up onstage. I am Cinderella, asking one of the prince's guards to dance.

"Cut," says Mr. Mooney. That means we can stop being our characters because Mr. Mooney wants to say something.

He walks to the edge of the stage and looks up at me. "First, you don't need to shout."

"I'm projecting," I say.

He nods. "Projecting and yelling are not the same thing. Also, Mary Margaret, can you show me where in the script Cinderella asks one of the prince's guards to dance?"

"Oh, that's easy," I say. "It's not in the script."

Mr. Mooney lifts his glasses and rubs his eyes. "Are you tired from all these tryouts?" I ask him.

"They are *auditions*," he says. His voice booms. "This is not some sports team. This is theater!" Then he says, "About your additions to the script . . ."

I know he's waiting for me to explain, so I do. "You said I should *be* Cinderella and to try to feel what she's feeling. Well, Cinderella is used to being dirty and wearing ugly stuff. But now all of a sudden she has this fancy dress and these dainty glass shoes. She looks kazowie beautiful—but she knows it's only until midnight, and then she'll have to wear rags again. She wouldn't just hang around waiting for the prince to ask her to dance. She'd want to dance with everyone."

"That's not the story," says Mr. Mooney.

"But it should be the story," I say. "It's more like real life."

"But it's not," he says. He is starting to sound a little cranky with me.

I think maybe he isn't understanding what I mean, so I explain some more. "Being Cinderella at that ball would be like being at Baskin-Robbins with all those kinds of ice cream—chocolate, strawberry, blue moon, Superman, rocky road—and you could eat from any of those. As much as you wanted! Or you could just stand there—ho, hum—and wait until the lady makes you a vanilla cone. Which would you do?"

Suddenly all the kids are talking about how great that would be, and what their favorite flavor is, and what they'd try first, and what kind of cones they would order—waffle or plain or sugar.

Mr. Mooney lets everyone talk for a minute and then says, "Quiet on the set!" He looks at me. "I understand what you're saying," he says. "And your interpretation would be interesting to do sometime, but for *this* production we'll be sticking to the script. Read your lines, please, and only your lines."

I don't say anything. I just sort of flounce back to my place onstage. *Sticking to the script* was what Ellie had done when she tried out before me. And to me it was yawnfully boring.

"Let's try the scene at the bottom of page seventy— where the prince puts the slipper on Cinderella's foot."

I sit down on a stool, and the prince kneels in front of me. "I've found her," he mumbles to my foot.

"Say it with a little feeling, like you've just found your long-lost baseball glove."

"I don't play baseball," he says.

"Then say it like you just found a ten-dollar bill."

"Oh, okay. Woo-hoo! I FOUND HER!" he says, but he still says it to my foot. "Summon all the people in the land. I've found some money—uhh, I mean *my princess*, and we'll marry on the morrow."

The two mean stepsisters pretend to be surprised. I flounce over to them and stick out my tongue. "So there!" I say to them. That cracks everyone up, and even Mr. Mooney smiles a little, like he can't help it. He's scribbling something on his clipboard. I'm pretty sure that means I'll be getting the part of Cinderella. Ellie said all the lines right, but Mr. Mooney had to tell her to speak up. And he wasn't smiling when she got offstage, the way he's smiling now. His smile will be even bigger on opening night, when he sees me up onstage all by myself. Well, the stepsisters and prince will be there, too, but I'll be the one he notices. I am the great *Mary Marguerite!* I am his star.

Mr. Mooney says that the cast list will be posted on Monday afternoon. The weekend drags. By Sunday, I'm asking my mother what time it is so much that she finally just starts announcing it all the time. "Two ten!" she yells from the bathroom. "Two twenty," she says as she walks through the living room. "Two twenty-one," she says when she walks through again, a minute later.

"Very funny," I say.

"Time goes faster when you're doing something," she says. "Distract yourself. Don't you have any homework?"

I settle down with a pen and paper to write another haiku. Nature, I think. Na-ture, na-ture, na-ture. But another part of my brain is thinking, Cinderella, Cinderella, Cinderella, and I can't get that part of my brain to be quiet. Fortunately, there is some nature in Cinderella.

Haiku #11
Magic orange pumpkin
BANG! Explodes in white moonlight
Now it's a carriage

Next I get a piece of lettuce and go out to play with Hershey. I take her out of her cage and put her on the lawn. I'm teaching her to roll over, but so far it doesn't seem like she is very smart. I wave the lettuce over her head, but she just looks at me with her big brown eyes and blinks. Then she hops away and nibbles on grass. Finally, I get tired of that. I do what I always do after we're done playing. I lie down on the grass and make a kissing sound to get her attention. Then I put a raisin between my lips. She hops over and takes the raisin from me. It's the way I tell her I love her, even though she's not a dog, which is what I really want, or a genius bunny.

After dinner, I try to read a book, but I'm too jangled up. JT and his friend Duff are goofing around on the computer. JT and Duff aren't best buds the way they used to be, but they are still friends. JT has a dictionary on the computer, and when he clicks on a word, the computer says it out loud. Duff clicks on a word. "Flatulence," the computer says in a lady's voice. She says the word very seriously, like a teacher. Duff clicks on it again and again, so the lady says, "Flatulence. Flatulence. Flatulence." This is cracking Duff and JT up.

"What's flatulence?" I ask. Duff tries to tell me, but he is laughing so hard that he can't get the words out. Finally he holds up his pointer finger, then types something else into the computer.

"Fart," says the lady in the computer. "Fart. Fart."

"Flatulence means fart?" I ask.

"They're related," Duff says. "Farts are caused by flatulence."

"Hey," I say. "Want to see what I can do?"

"Do we have a choice?" JT asks.

I crook one arm like a wing and then slip my other hand under my shirt into my underarm. Then I flap my arm a couple of times hard. *Fhhhpt! Fhhpt! FHHHH-PPPPT!* goes my underarm.

"Nice one," says JT. He taught me that, but now I can do it even better than him. He doesn't practice as much as I do.

Just then the computer dings. JT clicks around on it for a minute and then says, "Huh! I can't believe it." He double-clicks, and a picture of Caleb Strong comes onto the computer screen. "Caleb Strong actually sent you an e-mail," says JT.

"Let me see! Let me see!" I say, shoving my face closer to the screen. When I do that, I can see that Caleb is holding a ferret in one hand and a sign that says, "Make the Sunnydale Stage Door Players Your Pet Project" in the other. "What did he say?" I ask. "Did he say anything?"

"Get out of the way, and I'll tell you," he says, leaning into me with his shoulder.

"Sorry, I'm just so excited."

JT reads the e-mail.

Dear Mary Margaret: Your project sounds cool and I'm glad to be able to help. Here's a picture of me with my pet ferret, Harrison, that you can use for your calendar. And I DO remember what it was like to act for fun. You're pretty smart for a nine-year-old. See you at the movies!

P.S. My ferret uses a litter box so I don't need a #2 Tote, but thanks anyway.

"Caleb Strong said yes!" I yell. "He said YES!" I throw my arms around JT and give him a big hug, and then I hug Duff, too, just because he's standing in the way of my hugging arms. I jump around the room, swinging my arms like a monkey who ate five pieces of birthday cake. JT and Duff are pointing at me and laughing, but I don't care. "Mr. Mooney was wrong!" I sing. "There was enough time for my great idea! I did it! I did it!"

"Thanks to me," says JT.

I stop spinning. "Huh?" I say.

"You did it thanks to me. Remember? It was my idea to use e-mail, and then I found the address."

"Oh, right. Thanks, JT," I say. "Thanks a lot. You're the best big brother ever!" I start to come over to give him another hug, but he dodges me by rolling away in the desk chair.

"Okay, okay, Mary Mushy." Then he and Duff go to the kitchen for some leftover pizza.

I sit down in the chair and stare at Caleb Strong. I don't get stupid crazy over movie stars, and he doesn't even look like a movie star. He's wearing what my mother would call a ratty old T-shirt, and he has a goofy grin on his face. He's holding Harrison right against his stomach. Suddenly I feel like I have to kiss him, and so I put my lips on the computer screen and kiss him right on his sweet furry face. "Thank you, Harrison Ferret," I whisper. "Thank you for being Caleb Strong's pet." And then I whisper a thank-you to Caleb Strong, too, because he's actually the one who sent the e-mail. But I don't kiss Caleb Strong because that would be gross!

But maybe I should, because now that I have his picture, we are going to sell a bazillion calendars, and we'll be able to put on the best play ever. And it was all my idea. I did it. I saved the show! I am a hero. So now of course I'll get the part I want, because without me there wouldn't even BE a show. I deserve it.

"Uh, that's not exactly the way it works," says Andy the next morning on the bus. I am showing him the picture of Caleb Strong and Harrison. JT helped me print it from the computer. I'm going to give it to Mr. Mooney when I get to school.

"What are you talking about?" I say. "That's what's fair."

"Maybe it's different in a play, but in an orchestra, the person who is best at playing the instrument gets to play the solo."

"Well, this is different."

"How?" Andy asks.

"I don't know. It just is." I am starting to get a little frustrated that he is not agreeing with me. "Besides, I am the best at acting, so that will work out good."

"Better than Ellie?" he asks.

I look out the window and watch the houses bump by. "Pretty better," I say. I'm glad that Andy can't feel the tiny twitch in my mind that says Mr. Mooney might not think so.

When I show Mr. Mooney the picture of Caleb Strong, he pats me on the back and says, "Well done! I'm glad you went ahead and tried, even though I told you we didn't have time. I bet we'll be able to sell twice as many calendars because of this."

Ellie comes over right then. "Pardon me, Mr. Mooney" —she actually says that, *pardon me*. Ugh—"what would you like me to do with my report on women of the Revolutionary War?" She holds up something that looks like a book. The pages have typing on them, and the cover has that plastic stuff on it, kind of like plastic has been ironed onto it. My report is on dogs in the Revolutionary War. At least that's what it's going to be about. I haven't actually started writing it yet.

"Ellie, that's not due until the end of next week," he says.

"I didn't want it to be late," she says. "Is it okay if I turn it in now?"

I roll my eyes, but then I then I think I should be nice to her. She is going to be crushed when she finds out she doesn't get to play Cinderella. "Nice report," I say. I grit my teeth together and pull my lips apart and hope she thinks it's a smile.

"Thanks," she says. She seems really glad I noticed her report. "Is that a photograph of Caleb Strong?"

"Yeah, I asked him to be in our calendar, and he said yes."

"*You* did that?"

"Yes, she did," says Mr. Mooney. "All by herself."

I know it's not polite to correct a teacher, especially on stuff that's not really important, so I don't tell him that JT helped me.

"Wow," she says. "Congratulations." She says it like she means it. I wish she would stop being so nice all the time. It makes it really hard to not like her. "Even if I did get a great idea like that," she says, "I don't think I would have tried it."

"Why not?"

She looks at me with big blue eyes. "Because I would have been sure he'd say no. I mean, he's a *movie star*."

"But he said yes."

"But what if he said no? That would feel like . . . flunking or something."

I don't get what she's saying. "But he said yes," I say again.

"But he could have said no," she says.

"So what?" I say.

"It's never a mistake to try," says Mr. Mooney.

But that's not the way I feel at the end of the day, when Mr. Mooney puts up the list of who got which part. Because I tried out—I mean *auditioned*—to be Cinderella, and I put my whole heart right into that, but next to the word *Cinderella* is . . . *Ellie*. Ellie! I read down the list, looking for my name. I finally find it next to the words *Prince's Servant*. For a minute, that is a big relief to me. Maybe someone just made a little goof. Everyone knows the prince's servant is a boy, so why would my name be next to a boy's part?

I look around for Mr. Mooney. Everybody is very excited, talking to each other about which part they got, so it is very noisy. I see Mr. Mooney on the other side of the room. He is sitting by himself, writing stuff on his clipboard. I walk over to him very calm. "Mr. Mooney," I say, "I think someone goofed."

He pushes his glasses up on top of his head. "Oh?" he says.

"Yeah, and it's a funny one. Someone put my name next to *Prince's Servant*. How could anyone put my name, which is actually two girl names—Mary plus Margaret—next to a boy's part?"

He flips through the pages on his clipboard until he comes to the list. "No," he says. "There's no mistake. I did cast you as the prince's servant."

"You did?" I am confused, like when I wake up in the middle of the night when I'm at a sleepover, and I don't remember where I am. "But there are two things that are wrong about that. First, I'm not a boy. And second, I tried out for Cinderella."

"You can play a boy's part. Actors do it all the time."

"But I don't want to be the servant," I say. "I want to be Cinderella." My face feels hot. "This is . . . it's . . . it's *unacceptable*," I sputter. "It's not fair!"

Now Mr. Mooney looks confused. "Why do you think that?"

"Because I came up with the idea for the calendar, and I got JT to agree to do it, and then I even got Caleb Strong. Without me, there wouldn't even be a play!"

"I see," he says. He sighs and pats the seat beside him. "Sit down for a minute." I do. "I know you wanted to be Cinderella, but I decided to give the part to Ellie."

"Why? She can't even pronunciate!" I say.

"She'll get better, at *pro*jecting and *e*nunciating," he says. "Those are things you can learn. You did a good job at those things, but you kept saying lines that weren't in the script. And you *liked* changing them, didn't you?"

I lift my chin and nod. I *did* like changing them. I liked changing them because my lines were better. Everyone thought so, except Mr. Mooney.

"Cinderella is the main part," he says. "I need to be able to trust whoever is in the lead to follow the script."

"But what about all that stuff you said? All that stuff about how the character has to be in your heart? Cinderella *is* in my heart! I *know* she is! I can feel what she's feeling!"

Mr. Mooney looks at me a little sadly. "No, Mary Margaret. When you were auditioning for Cinderella, you were feeling what *you* would feel. You were reacting the way Mary Margaret would if she were at a ball. I love Mary Margaret—I love the way she never gives up, I love her boldness—but for this play I need a Cinderella."

I don't care that there are some things Mr. Mooney loves about me. He doesn't love me enough to make me Cinderella, and that's all that matters. I am mad times ten—mad times a hundred, even. "It's not fair!" I say. It's getting hard to see because my eyes are full of tears. "I don't want to be the measly old servant. He only says about two words for the whole play!"

"It's a fine place to start," says Mr. Mooney. "If you do it and do it well, next year you'll be ready for something bigger."

"I'm ready for something bigger now, if you'll just give me the chance!" I jump up so fast that I kind of stumble into Mr. Mooney, and his clipboard falls to the floor. Part of me is sorry, but most of me is glad. "Please! Please! I'll do anything," I say. And I mean it. I would do anything.

"I stand by my decision," he says. "You're free to refuse the servant part if you wish, but I hope you'll take it."

I'm in such a big hurry to get to the door that I bump into a bunch of kids. They want to talk about me and Caleb Strong, but I don't care about him or the calendar or the play anymore, and I keep going. I'm almost to the door when I see someone sitting alone, kind of hunched over. Her hair is hiding her face, and her shoulders are jerking a little bit. It might be Ellie, but I'm not sure. By then my tears are making everything blurry.

I slam the door when I get home. JT is at the computer. "Hello!" the dictionary lady's voice says. "Hello! Hello!" I know he's trying to be funny. But when he sees my face, he stops. That's the nice thing about JT. He usually knows when to stop, which is something I'm not that good at. "What happened?" he asks. "What's wrong?"

"I didn't get the part!" I yell. "After all that stuff I did, and I still didn't get it. Ellie got it."

"Mr. Mooney thought she was better at acting?"

"He thinks she's better at everything!" I say. "Every little thing. Every big thing. Every in-between thing. And now she has what I wanted more than anything. She's perfect! But I think she's . . . she's . . ." I elbow JT out of the way and type the letters S-T-O-O-P-I-D into the computer while he watches.

"I'm sorry," says the lady's voice. "I don't recognize that word. Please check the spelling and try again."

"Errrrrgh!" I yell. "I can't even get that right!" I turn around and start crying again.

"That's only because you're upset," says JT. "You need a U instead of two O's." I hear him typing, then he asks, "Is this what you wanted to say about Ellie?" he asks. Then the lady's voice says, "Stupid. Stupid. Stupid."

And even though that was exactly what I wanted to say, hearing it just makes me cry harder.

JT is a good brother, but even he doesn't know how to fix me when my body is a crying lump of Jell-O on the floor. He goes to find Mom. She gets right down on the floor next to me. Her arms are empty of Baby Liza, and so I fill them up with me. "I . . . didn't get . . . the part," I say into her shoulder. It's hard to talk because the crying makes my voice jiggle.

"I know," she says. "I'm sorry." She lays her cheek on the top of my head and just holds me while I cry. Finally I am all cried out, and my body goes limp like a wet swimsuit.

"I am not Cinderella," I say.

My mom puts her hand under my chin and lifts my face up so her eyes and my eyes are staring at each other. "You are to me, Loverly," she says.

I know my mom is trying to make me feel better, and it works—for about a minute. "Yeah, but you're just my mom."

"Just?" she says, giving me a little tickle under my arms. *"Just?"*

"Don't, Mom," I say. I am not ready to be joked out of my bad mood yet. "I really want to be Cinderella. But stup—" I stop myself just in time. "But that Ellie got the part."

She nods and rocks me back and forth for a while. My mom can't always make my bad feelings go away, but she's good at keeping me company while I have them. We're both just quiet for a little while. Then she says, "Do you really *really* want to be Cinderella?"

"Uh-huh, really."

"Because there might still be a way."

"You mean, in the play?"

"It would kind of be in the play, but not exactly. And I don't know if Mr. Mooney will let you do it. Sometimes there's an understudy for the leading role—someone who learns all the lines and practices onstage in case something happens to the star."

I sniffle one last time and look up at her. I feel like there is a little slice of sunshine in my heart. "Really? Like if the star is just out walking her dog? And then BAM! a tree falls on her and breaks all her bones? Except the bones in the arm that was holding the leash?"

My mom pushes her eyebrows together the way she does when she's worried about me getting sick. "Well, more often what happens is the star gets a cold or the flu," she says. "But—and I want you to listen closely, Mary Margaret—most of the time the understudy doesn't get to perform in front of an audience."

"Then why would anyone do it?"

"Because they love acting and want to learn how to be better at it."

"So they never get to be up in front of people?"

"Hardly ever. This is something you'd do because you want a chance to play Cinderella and not because you want to be up in front of everyone."

"Oh," I say, and then I get quiet. I am thinking.

"Mary Margaret," my mom says. "Do you understand what I'm saying?"

I nod. I am still thinking. I am thinking that "hardly ever" does not mean "never ever."

My mom and me have been together since the day I was born, so she knows me pretty good. She says, "Repeat after me: If I'm an understudy . . ."

It seems silly to say the same thing she's saying. "Mo-om, I get it," I say.

She squinches up her eyes at me. *"If I'm an understudy . . ."* she says in her I-mean-business voice.

I can tell that she's not going to change her mind, and I'm too limpish from crying to fight about it. So this is the way our little talk goes.

Me: "If I'm an understudy . . ."

Her: "It is *extremely* unlikely . . ."

Me: "It is *extremely* unlikely . . ."

Her: "That I'll get to perform in front of an audience."

Me: "That I'll get to perform in front of an audience."

Her: "Good."

She gives me one last hug, and I do something I was positive I'd never do again. I smile. I smile because I am remembering how once, when I was five and not very smart yet, I begged to have a little sister, and my mother said to me, "That is *extremely* unlikely." But now I have one—Liza. So *extremely unlikely* means that there's a chance I could still get to be Cinderella, up onstage, in front of everyone. Even if it's only a tiny chance, it's still a chance. And me + a chance = hope.

The next day I ask Mr. Mooney if I can be an understudy.

"You want to be Ellie's understudy?"

I haven't actually thought about it this way—being *Ellie's* understudy. But it's the only way I have a chance to get what I want. I take a deep breath and say, "Yes."

"Why?"

I think back to what my mom said about why I *should* want to be an understudy. I know that is the answer I have to give Mr. Mooney. "Because I want to be Cinderella and to learn to be better at acting," I say.

"If you were the prince's servant, you'd at least get to be onstage during a real performance," he says. "If you do this, you probably won't ever get to be onstage. You realize that, right?"

"Right," I say. "It is extremely unlikely."

"Extremely," he says.

I nod. "It almost never happens. I know."

"But if you're an understudy, then I would have a new problem," he says. "I need a new prince's servant. Do you have any ideas?"

A name springs into my brain. "Stevie Butts," I say. "He'd make a perfect prince's servant."

"Do you think he'd want to?"

"Sure," I say, even though I don't know.

He stares at me and doesn't say anything. For a minute I think he's going to say "No." But then he says, "Okay. If you can get a replacement for your part, then you can be an understudy." He digs into a box behind his desk and gives me a script. "One of a kind, as usual," he says.

"The script?" I ask.

"No, you," he says. He smiles at me just like he used to before that Ellie came. "I know this is hard for you. I'm glad you found a way to be part of the play, even though you aren't going to have the lead."

Yet, I think. Because I am thinking I don't have the lead yet. But I guess I say "Yet" out loud by mistake because then Mr. Mooney says, "Pardon me?"

"Uh . . . I said *yes! Yes*, I'm glad I found a way, too!"

That night while I'm playing with Hershey, I tell her about how I'm going to play Cinderella and how maybe she can come watch me. *Maybe she could even be in the play!* She could play the animal that the fairy godmother turns into the footman on the coach! I'll have to talk to Mr. Mooney about that.

"There's some stuff I need to do before that, though," I say to her. "I have to convince Stevie Butts to be in the play. That will be easy. And I have to practice hard so I know all my lines, so I'm ready to be Mary Marguer-*ite*, the star!" I make the kissing noise and put a raisin between my lips. Hershey hops over. I feel her whiskers against my lips when she takes it. I don't tell her what I am thinking right then—that the last thing I have to do is hope that something happens to Ellie so she can't be Cinderella.

Because when you wish for something rotten like that, you don't tell your best friend, even if she is a rabbit.

Crunch, crunch, cruuunch. Stevie Butts is eating the "ants in snow" that I brought for him—celery + Cool Whip + dried cranberries = ants in snow. It's kind of like "bugs on a log," which is celery + peanut butter + raisins, but Stevie Butts is allergic to peanuts, so I thought up this especially for him.

"Mmm-mmm-mmm," he says. He licks the Cool Whip, which is kind of runny because it's warm, off his fingers. "I think it would be better if you added some chocolate chips."

I zip my lunch box back up and put it in my backpack. "So it would be 'ants and rocks in snow.'"

74

He giggles. "Or 'ants and poop in snow.'"

Stevie *Butts* said *poop*. That makes me laugh so extremely that I almost pee my pants.

"So do you want to be in the play or not?" I ask him when I am my normal self again. I told him about everything right away when I got on the bus, but I could tell he wasn't listening back then. I could tell he wasn't going to be good for the listening part of the bus ride until he was finished with the eating part.

"Uh, I don't know, Mary Margaret. What if I'm no good?"

I put my backpack under my seat and swipe one hand across the other. This is what my mother does when it is time to "get down to business."

I say, "Well, let's see right now if you are or not. Say, 'This way, sire!'"

He clears his throat. "This way, sire!"

He spits a little on the word *sire*. I hope the prince's servant doesn't ever have to stand too close to Cinderella because I don't want to get spit on. "Great!" I say, because I want him to be in the play. "Are you sure you haven't acted before?"

Stevie Butts, who is excellent at slouching, sits up a little straighter. "Uh-uh."

"Wow. You could be really good at it. There's one more line. Say 'As you wish, sire!'"

Stevie Butts is getting kind of excited about being a

servant. He jumps up in the aisle of the bus and shouts, "AS YOU WISH, SIRE!"

All the other kids laugh, and then from the front of the bus, the bus driver says in a growly voice, "What I wisheth is that thee would placeth thy bottom on the seat."

Stevie Butts blushes and sits down. "Okay," he says to me. "If you think I'm good, I'll do it."

That afternoon, I am excited to practice my lines at home. But even before I open the door, I can hear Liza, and she is doing what she does best—crying. My dad says that Liza has turned our house into a crying factory. "Cries?" he says, when I walk through the kitchen. "You need 'em? We got 'em! Loud cries, soft cries, whimpers, and yells. We got 'em all, and they are priced to sell. We're running a special on shrieks this afternoon. Two for the price of a smile. You interested?"

"No," I say, dropping my backpack on the table and clapping my hands over my ears. "Why can't you just put tape over her mouth?" I say.

"We've been through all that, Mary Margaret," says my dad. "You know we tested all kinds of tape, and there just isn't one strong enough to keep our little Liza's lips together." He's joking. They haven't really tried taping her mouth closed.

I pull the script out of my backpack and tell him that

I'm going to Andy's. I hope that he's there. I find him in the backyard, playing fetch with Itzy.

"Where were you?" I ask, because he wasn't on the bus, and it's not a violin lesson day.

"At the dentist." He throws the tennis ball. It bounces off a tree. Andy is excellent at the violin but not so good at anything sporty. That's why I think the tie he's wearing today is kind of funny. It has golf clubs on it.

Itzy runs the ball back to us. "Is that a new tie?" I ask.

"Yeah. My grandpa bought it for me, so my mom says I have to wear it sometimes." Andy pulls his arm back to throw the ball again.

"I guess he wants you to play golf, huh?"

Andy drops his arm to his side and scratches his forehead. "I don't know. Do you think so? He does play golf."

"Haven't you ever heard of 'dropping a hint'?" I say.

"I guess, but I didn't think a tie could be a hint." Andy throws the ball again. It bounces off the basement window. Good thing he doesn't throw very hard.

"Mr. Mooney said I can be an understudy for Cinderella." I hold up my script. "Want to help me practice?"

We read through some parts of the play. I remember to pronunciate very loudly. Mr. Mooney says we should use our whole bodies to act, so I also wave my arms around a lot. I use my whole body so well that once I accidentally whap Andy right on the cheek. He is looking at his script, so he doesn't see my arm come flying toward his face.

"Owww!" he says.

"Sorry!" I say.

"You've been doing that the whole time."

"No, I haven't. That's the only time I hit you."

"I don't mean hitting. I mean being showy."

"What do you mean, *showy*?"

"Like in an orchestra—if you make big movements with the bow when no one else is or if you move too much with the music—that's showy. Anything that makes the audience look at just you."

"But Cinderella is the star. Everyone is *supposed* to look at me."

Andy looks like he isn't so sure. "I don't think the play is just about you, even if you are the star," he says. "People go to plays because they like to hear a story."

"Yeah, so?"

"It takes a lot of people to tell the story. Just like it takes a lot of musicians to play a symphony. Not just one violinist, no matter how good he is. If just the violin played a symphony, it wouldn't work. The violin part sounds dumb without all the other parts."

"But-but-but," I say, trying to think of what to say next because, according to me, I am *good* at acting, and now Andy is kind of telling me I'm not. "But the name of the play is *Cinderella*. That's me. And there aren't any symphonies called *Violin*, are there?"

"No," he says. "But—"

"See? This is different than your old orchestra." I am pretty sure that it is. About ninety-eight percent sure, which is almost completely sure.

And that is sure enough for me.

On the first day of play practice, JT is acting weird before he leaves for school. He's asking me all kinds of questions. Then he acts like he's not even interested in the answers. If he's not, then why is he asking me questions? That's what I would like to know.

"How long will play practice be?" He has half of his headphones on, and he's sway-rocking to the music.

"A couple of hours."

He turns the music down. "Oh. Who is going to be there?"

"I don't know. Everybody."

"Yeah, but just the actors? Or the crew, or what?"

I shrug. "All I know is that I have to be there."

Then he says, "If you, you know, see Claire—that girl who we saw at the first meeting?—could you give this to her?" He pushes a folded-up piece of paper across the table to me, trying to pretend that he asks me to give notes to girls all the time. Which he does not. Because (A) girls are annoying, (2) he thinks they have cooties, and (last-ish) I am famous in my family for my natural curiosity. That is what my dad calls it—natural curiosity. JT calls it snooping. I like what my dad calls it better.

I pick the note up. "It's not in a licked envelope."

JT pulls on a sweatshirt. "Nope. It's not even in an unlicked envelope. Which means I'm trusting you. What do you think? Should I trust you?"

I think about how long it has been since the last time I snooped. It's been a few days, at least, which means I've probably broken the snooping habit. "Sure!" I say.

"That would be nice," says JT. "So you'll give it to her, right, Mary Mailgirl? And you won't read it first?"

"Right."

After JT leaves, I turn the note over to see if it's booby-trapped in some way. Like maybe if I open it, it will spray ink all over me, or an alarm will go off. It doesn't look like it's booby-trapped. It's just folded so that it will stay closed by itself, without tape or anything.

I shove the note in the pocket of my pants. All day while I'm at school I try to forget about that note. I try to think about play practice instead. And once in a while (because I am in school) I have to think about things like how I wish that the *i*'s and *e*'s would stop trading places in words like *believe* and *receive*. Ellie always knows where the *i* and the *e* belong. That's because her name has so many of them, and I only have that one measly *e* in my name and no *i*'s at all. But just wait until we get words that have the same letters as *my* name in them. Words like *maggot* or *malamute* or *Madagascar*. I'm pretty sure there aren't any *i*'s or *e*'s in Madagascar.

So I keep trying to forget about that note, but all day it keeps poking at me. Like my neighbor Jolene pokes at me when she wants to me to notice her. "Hey," she says, poking me in the arm. "Hey! Want to know something?" *Poke, poke.* "Guess what?" *Poke, poke, poke.* She does that until you *have* to answer her or slug her just to get her to stop poking.

That's what that note is doing, too. It has a pokey edge, and every time I sit down, it pokes me. It's like the note is trying to talk to me. "Look at me!" it says. "I'm still here! Read me! No one would have to know." But each time my hand starts creeping in there, I pull it back out. I am working on not being so naturally curious.

By the time I get to practice in the afternoon, I can't wait to find Claire and get rid of that note before it talks me into reading it. But before I can find her, Mr. Mooney calls us all to the stage.

"We're going to go through every scene so that each of you knows where to stand," he says. "It's called blocking. Cinderella? Where's my Cinderella?" he calls.

"Here!" Ellie and I say at the same time. I say it because I am *a* Cinderella.

"Oh, yes! My Cinderella and my Cinderella Two. There's going to be so much to remember for that role.

Mary Margaret, why don't you take notes that you both can use? That way Cinderella can better listen to my directions."

"I said I didn't want to be the prince's servant, and I don't want to be *anyone's* servant," I grumble. Mr. Mooney doesn't hear me, but Ellie does.

She reaches for the paper and pencil. "I'll take the notes, Mary Margaret," she says. "I don't mind."

Oh, no, you don't, I think. You're going to be great at blocking *and* at taking notes, and Mr. Mooney will love you even more than he already does. But I know that trick, and I won't let her do it on me.

"No, that's okay. He asked me to do it," I say.

Mr. Mooney blocks us for a long time. "Stand to the right of center," he says. And "Stand to the left of center." And "Everyone! If someone is standing in front of you when it's time to say your lines, step *out* and step *up*. The audience needs to be able to see and hear you!"

When we get to the part where the fairy godmother comes in, the Fairy Godmother is missing. Mr. Mooney looks at his clipboard. "Zoe? Is Zoe Evans here?" Suddenly a lady clomps onto the stage. "She'll be right here," she says, panting. "She's just changing out of her cleats. We came from soccer practice."

Mr. Mooney looks at her over his glasses. It's the kind of look that means DON'T LET THIS HAPPEN AGAIN. "She has a very important part," he says. "Without her fairy godmother, Cinderella won't make it to the ball. If she doesn't make it to the ball, she can't dance with the prince, and then he wouldn't fall in love with her, and there wouldn't be a happy ending. We don't want that, now, do we?"

"We run a little late sometimes," says the lady, "but she doesn't have practice at night, so she'll be here on time for the play."

Mr. Mooney sighs. "Let's move on, then," he says. "Steven! Where's Steven?"

No one says anything.

"Don't tell me that another cast member is late," says Mr. Mooney. "Mr. Steven Butts!"

"Oh!" says Stevie Butts. "I didn't know you were calling me."

"Steven is your name, is it not?" says Mr. Mooney.

"Yes, but I'm used to Stevie Butts."

"Well, here you'll be either Steven or Prince's Servant."

Stevie Butts nods. "Okay." He whispers the name to himself. "Steven. Steven."

"Now, your trademark is going to be a bow," says Mr. Mooney. "You'll be doing a lot of bowing. We'll have to experiment with exactly when you'll bow. If we get the timing right, you'll get a lot of laughs."

Stevie Butts takes a very big bow. So big that his hand hits the ground. Everyone laughs. "Hey," he says. "You're right!"

The whole time, I stick to Ellie like fleas stick to a dog, which is what Mr. Mooney said to do. Only he didn't say that fleas on the dog part. Every time he tells her where to stand in a scene, she says, "Oh, sorry!" I don't know why she does that. It's the first time he's ever even told us where to stand, so it's not like she made a mistake.

Finally, practice is over. Ellie smiles at me. "I think it's neat you're a Cinderella, too," she says.

"You do?"

"Yes. It's kind of like having a sister. Or maybe even a twin," she says.

She is kind of like Liza, because she is in my way. Before my sister was born, she had what I wanted more than anything—my mom. And now *Ellie* has what I want more than anything. But this time, I can do something about it.

"Are you nervous about being the star?" I ask. "I mean, you'll probably be great at it and everything. It's just . . . if you flub up, you know, the whole play would be a flop probably. Some actors get really nervous and can't even go onstage." Andy told me that when he helped me practice my lines. He said the same thing happens with musicians sometimes.

"I've had butterflies before," says Ellie. "Everyone does a little bit."

"This isn't normal butterflies," I say. "This is different. Stage fright is more like snarling, flying dinosaurs racing around your stomach than like friendly flitting butterflies. That's how bad it is."

Ellie twirls some hair tight around her finger. "You must mean pterosaurs," she says. "The flying reptiles."

"Yeah, that's what I mean. Those ptero-thingies," I say. But I think, Does she have to know everything? "But if that happened, it wouldn't be too much of a disaster. Because I could go on for you. The show must go on, just like Mr. Mooney always says. So don't worry about that stage fright thing. It doesn't happen very often. When it does—*oooooo-weeee!* But I'm sure it won't happen to you. I'm sure you'll get up onstage in front of those thousands of people—"

"Thousands?"

"I think, yeah. But that won't bother you at all. And neither will the spotlight shining right in your eyes. And I'm sure you'll remember all your lines, even though they all sound kind of alike, and you'll always remember who you're supposed to say them to. You'll be great!"

"Of course she'll be great!" says a voice behind me.

"Hi, Mom," says Ellie. "Mary Margaret, this is my mom. Mom, this is Mary Margaret. She's learning the part of Cinderella, too." I notice that Ellie didn't say "She's my understudy," which would have made me feel like a servant again or like the way Cinderella feels when the stepsisters order her around.

Her mom sticks out her hand so I can shake it. It's bony and cold, so I let go of it after half a shake. "So you're Ellie's understudy?" she says.

I was right. When she calls me *Ellie's understudy*, it makes me feel low-down.

I don't say anything. Everyone else might think I'm Ellie's understudy, but underneath that, I'm really Cinderella. It's just like everyone thinks Cinderella is a maid— until her fairy godmother comes along. I'm just waiting for something like a fairy godmother to come along and— *poof!*—make Ellie disappear.

"Am I late?" asks Ellie. Her shoulders are kind of hunched around her face. It makes her look like she's shrinking. The Incredible Shrinking Ellie! Maybe she'll shrink up and blow away.

"Just a tad," says her mother. "Shoulders back, dear. Slouching is so unbecoming on a young lady."

Ellie's shoulders go back. "Sorry."

"That's a good girl," her mom says. "Did you hand in your report?"

"Yes," says Ellie.

Ellie's mom straightens Ellie's headband. "Do your accelerated reading program?"

"Yes," she says. Ellie is just standing there, letting her mom fuss at her. The last time my mom tried any of that stuff with me, I was ducking and bobbing like crazy. It worked, too. She never did manage to get a hand on my pokey-uppy hair.

"And how did the timed math quiz go today?"

"I got forty-eight out of fifty right."

Ellie's mom puts on a big pout—bigger even than my neighbor Jolene, who is spoiled and has had a lot of practice pouting. "Well, someone must have been distracting you. I'm sure you know all the answers." And then Ellie's mom says to me, "She's our only child—that way we can give her every opportunity. She just seems to be naturally gifted at everything she tries." She smiles down at Ellie. "She's our perfect girl."

It looks like Ellie's mom could keep talking and talking, but Ellie is pulling her away. "Come on, Mom. I'm ready to go now. Bye, Mary Margaret."

"Nice meeting you," says her mother.

Everyone else is leaving, too. I sprawl across a couple of seats while I wait for my mom to pick me up. "Ellie is our perfect girl!" I say in a high, singsong voice, but quietly. "Ellie is naturally gifted." Big deal. Just then I feel a poke in my thigh. It's that stupid note again. And then I think that I'm naturally gifted, too. I have a natural gift for being curious. I feel a little guilty, because JT trusted me. But then I think it's not really my fault that I'm opening it. I didn't open the note all through school and all through play practice. That's way longer than I've ever gone, so I guess you could say I'm improving. My parents always tell me to do my best. And nine hours, fourteen minutes is definitely my best.

So I open the note. It says: HS CSY PMOI TYDDPIW? —NX

I can't read it, but I know what it means. It means that

JT thinks he is *so* smart. He knew I'd open it, but he was wrong. Actually, he *would have been* wrong, except for the little problem that the note kept poking me. *Everyone* thinks they are so smart. JT and Ellie—or at least Ellie's mother thinks Ellie is smart. But I have news for them. I am smart, too. I look at that note. I know the letters somehow make words. But how? I can figure it out if only . . .

But just then I see Claire, way across the room. Walking. *Toward me!* I do the only thing I can. I scribble the letters on my hand, then fold up the note. "Here!" I say, when she walks by. "It's from my brother." She's carrying a big stack of books that is kind of balanced against her stomach, so I put the note on top of the books.

She looks at the note. "Your brother?"

"Remember? That day of the first meeting? When you were late and me and him were standing in the lobby?"

"Oh!" she says. "Yeah, I do remember."

There's no good place to put the books down, so she hands them to me. At the last minute, I remember to keep my fist closed so she can't see what I've written on my hand.

She gives me a funny look. "Is something wrong with your hand?"

"Uhhhhh . . . it's part of my character. I thought it would be interesting if Cinderella had a gimpy hand. You know? Just something different."

She nods. "Oh. That is . . . original."

I hold her books while she reads the note. She smiles

a funny little smile. It reminds me of the kind of smile my mom gets in December when she has "Christmas secrets." Claire says, "Have you read this?"

"No," I say. This is the mostly honest truth. In school, Mr. Mooney says that in order to really read, you have to understand what you read. And I definitely did not understand what I read. So I didn't really read it.

"It's in some sort of code."

"It *is*?" I say, like I am as surprised as she is.

She shoves the note into the back pocket of her jeans. I bet it won't poke her there. That must be one of the things you learn when you're a teenager—the best place to carry notes. "I wonder why he would write it in code," she says.

Suddenly I am very interested in my fingernails. "I don't know," I say, looking at them. "Are you going to write back?"

"I've never gotten a note in code before. It's strange. I kind of like it that I have to figure it out. What's your brother like?"

I could tell her that he's smart and a fast runner and an expert on the computer. I could tell her about how he helps my mom with Baby Liza. I could even tell her that he's pretty nice, for a big brother, and that he once helped me save a rabbit from drowning. If I were Most Excellent Ellie, I probably would say all those things so that Claire would like him. But I'm not Most Excellent Ellie. I'm

Mary Margaret, and I'm feeling mean. I say the worst thing I can think of.

"He's a P. D.S."

"A what?"

"P. D.S. Poopy-dingle-snot," I say. I don't tell her that I just made the word up. Or that it means "someone you love a lot but then he hurts your feelings so bad that you wish you didn't love him anymore, but you still do."

9. Backstage Brouhaha

Hey, you got an e-mail back from Daria—that guy who's running for governor," JT says to me a few days later. "Don't you want to see it?"

I hang up my jacket. I don't usually hang up my jacket unless someone specifically tells me to, but if I hang it up this time, it means I don't have to answer JT right away. I have been trying not to talk to JT since he sent that note. This is very hard to do because he lives in the same house with me. And because I like to talk. And because every day he asks me the same question. He says, "Got anything for me?" as soon as I get home from play practice. (In my head I hear Mr. Mooney say, "*Rehearsals*, not practice. This is not some sports team!") I know what JT means. He means did Claire send him a note back. The answer to that is no. So that is one word that I like saying to him. "No," I always say. Then he slumps a little in his chair, like he's a stuffed animal that lost some of his stuffing.

I don't want to talk to JT, but I am curious about what

Mr. Daria said. So I shrug and walk over to the computer so I can read the e-mail.

Dear Mary Margaret,

I am thrilled and delighted that you asked me and Hilary to be in your calendar. We are proud to be able to make a contribution to this stellar community-building effort that will undoubtedly strengthen our state and our country. Don't forget to tell your parents and teachers to **VOTE FOR FRED DARIA!**—the candidate who *dares to be different.*

Fred Daria

Then there's a picture of him and a bulldog. Both of them are wearing "DARIA FOR GOVERNOR" pins.

"That must be Hilary," JT says, looking at the dog. She's wearing a red, white, and blue collar. "We already have twelve pictures. We don't need another one. What do you want me to tell him?"

"Nothing," I say. First, I am trying not to talk to JT, and second, Mr. Daria seems so excited to be in our calendar that I don't want to tell him that now he won't be. I know what it's like to be really excited about something and then be disappointed when it doesn't happen.

"You have to tell him something," he says.

"Later," I say.

"All right," he says. "Hey, do you—"

"No!" I say all snappy, because I know what the rest

of the question is. "I didn't get any stupid note back from Claire."

JT gets that saggy look and then goes back to work on the computer. All last week he took pictures of the people with their pets. Now he's making the pictures into the "Famous to Us" calendar. A few days ago, Mr. Mooney said that lots of people have bought the calendars. "More than I ever dreamed!" he said. So it's kind of like I made his dream come true. I wish I could make *my* dream come true.

But so far I am still "Cindy Two." That's what Mr. Mooney calls me now. It's short for Cinderella, and the "two" is because I'm the understudy. I guess that he has forgotten that I don't like my name shortened. A substitute teacher tried calling me just Mary for a while. She said, "Mary Margaret is such a long name. I'll just use Mary." Later I told her I needed to go to the toy.

"Pardon me?" she said.

"You know, the toy," I said, pointing to my bottom. "The toy-let?"

The other kids started saying stuff like that, too. We shortened everything! Music was *moo*, and recess was *reese*. Then the principal came in, and someone said, "Hey, prince!" After that, the substitute teacher called me Mary Margaret. Mr. Mooney knows that story. I told him that story the first week of school, and he laughed. He said, "I will remember never to shorten your name, Mary Margaret." And he didn't, either, until now. *Cindy Two*. Ugh.

After I'm done not talking to JT, I go out to find Hershey. Lots of times I practice my lines with her because I want to be ready when my time on center stage comes. I pretend that she's the handsome prince. "Me? A princess?" I say to her, pretending that she's putting the glass slipper on my foot. "Oh, yes, I'll marry you!" And then I make kissing sounds, and she hops right over to me. "Ah!" I say, all joyful. "I've never *bean* so happy."

Mr. Mooney says it's supposed to be "been." "I've never *been* so happy, Cindy Two, not *bean*," he says. "Cinderella turns into a princess, not a British citizen, so leave out the accent." But I think that once she's really a princess, Cinderella would say *bean*. It sounds fancier that way.

The next day at practice, Mr. Mooney lets me do the part where Cinderella asks to go to the ball, and the stepsisters laugh at her. When I say my lines, I pronunciate. And I remember what he said about only saying what's in the script, so those are the only lines I say out loud. There are lots of other things I think Cinderella would say, but I keep those things in my head. Mr. Mooney says I'm doing a good job. He even smiles at me, but before his smile is even all the way warmed up, he says, "Okay, let's do it with Cinderella." I know what he means. He means the *real* Cinderella. And then Ellie does the scene.

I wait for his high-beam smile, because that's what she always gets. But this time he frowns and taps his clipboard with his pen. "Cinderella, I want this scene to be big—big voice, like this. 'I can't *go?* But all the maidens in the kingdom are to be invited!' And big arm movements to go with the big protestations," he says. He's been bossy before, but he's being extra bossy now. "This is no time to be a wallflower, Cinderella. If you don't make it big, the audience won't feel your frustration. You have to make them feel how much you want to go and how unfair it is that you don't get to go. Okay? Big! Big! **BIG!**"

By the time he's done bossing her, it's Ellie's eyes that are big, big, big.

Mr. Mooney sighs. "Okay, everyone. Take ten, then we'll come back and do Act Two."

I sit down at a table near the drinking fountain and try to crack JT's code. I've been thinking about it since I read the note. Claire hasn't been able to do it yet, either. "Tell your brother I'm trying," she said once. But I didn't because I'm still mad at him.

The first thing I tried was doing the whole code backwards. HS CSY PMOI TYDDPIW? —NX turned into XN WIPDDYT IOMP YSC SH, but it didn't make the letters turn into words.

"What are you doing?" asks Ellie.

I keep looking at the letters that don't make any sense. "Nothing," I say.

"Can I do it with you?"

After following her around onstage for two hours, I don't feel like being with her. "No, I like to do nothing alone."

"All rah-rah-right," she says. Then I hear this weird

little gurgle noise. It's Ellie. She's crying. As soon as I look up at her, she sits down. "I'm sorry," she sobs. "I'll leave in a minute."

Ellie is Cinderella. Everyone loves Ellie. Ellie is perfect. I don't know why she is crying. "What's wrong?" I ask.

"He yelled at me," she says.

"Who? Mr. Mooney?"

She nods. "Yeh-hes. I'm not used to being yelled at. No one ever yells at me."

"That wasn't yelling," I say. "He's just being bossy. That's his job. He's the director."

"No-ho," she says. "He hates me. Mr. Moo-*hoo-hoo-hoo*-ney ha-ha-hates me."

The crying is starting to annoy me. It annoys me enough that I will do almost anything to make it stop. Plus, her crying is making people look over at us. People like Claire. And if Claire comes over, I won't be able to work on the code. So I try to trick Ellie the way we trick Baby Liza at home by distracting her. "Look," I say. "This is written in a secret code."

Ellie sniffles. "What's it say?"

"I don't know," I say.

"Who wrote it?"

Ellie would probably spoil everything if I told her, so I say, "That's a secret, too."

She swipes her eyes with a tissue—she actually carries one with her all the time!—and leans over the table.

"Are the words backwards?" she asks.

"Tried it," I say. It makes me feel smart that I already thought of that.

"Oh." She concentrates for a minute, then says, "Maybe the whole thing is off by one letter. Like any As in the code are really Bs, and any Bs are Cs."

We try that, but that doesn't work, either.

"What if you just use every other letter?" she asks.

I write it out that way. HCYMIYDIN. She scrunches up her nose. "Let's break the word up." She writes HCY-MI-Y-DIN. "Maybe now we can sound it out. 'Has my why den?' Does that mean anything?"

I shake my head. "What if we use every other letter but start with the S this time?" I write S-S-POTDP-WX.

"Spotty picks," she says.

Sometimes words seem like toys to me because they are fun to play with. "Spotty picks, is you poedull wicks?" I say, just for fun. Suddenly I think that's the funniest sentence I have ever heard, and I'm laughing so hard that a blop of my spit falls onto the table. "Spotty picks, is you poedull wicks?"

Ellie smiles but keeps looking at the paper. Just then Stevie Butts walks up. He has his hands behind his back. "Hi, Stevie Butts," I say.

"It's Steven," he says, very stern-like. Then he says, "Ellie, do you think . . . would you . . ." He pulls his hands out from behind his back. There's a pen in one hand and an autograph book in the other. "Sign my autograph book?

I think you're going to be famous someday." He looks at her all *adoring* or something.

"I'm not that good," she says. "I'm really just starting to learn." *No kidding*, I think. "Did you hear the way Mr. Mooney just yelled at me?"

"Yeah, but it's not you. He yelled at me, too, because I keep dropping the glass slipper," says Stevie Butts. "Sign right here—right after *Mercedes Lucia Mercada*."

Ellie looks like she doesn't really want to sign, but she does.

"Thanks," he says. "Thanks a lot." Then he leaves.

Because I like that laughy feeling I was getting before Stevie Butts interrupted us, I say, "Spotty picks, is you poedull wicks?" again. "Don't you think that's hilarious?"

"Mmm-hmmm," she says. That's all. Just "mmm-hmmm."

All of a sudden I feel crabby at her. Because maybe she thinks she's too good to laugh now that she's signed some dumb autograph book. "Then why don't you laugh?" I ask.

"I don't know. I guess I want to figure out the code."

"It's not even your code," I say. "It's *my* code, and if I think it's funny, you could at least laugh with me."

"I don't have to laugh just because you say so," she says. "Everyone keeps telling me what to do—Mr. Mooney, my mom, everybody. But I don't have to listen to you." She presses her lips tight together, and her face is getting red.

I know that she's getting mad, but I like it. There is a little spike in my heart that wants to make her even more mad. And that little spike tells me what to say next. "I bet you're too perfect to laugh. You're probably worried you'd snort snot through your nose and mess up your perfect little . . ." I wave my hand at her dress. "Your perfect little petit four."

"For your information, I am not perfect," she says, standing up. "I hate it when people say I am."

I am not really listening. Now that she's mad, I am thinking about what I will say next to make her stay mad. I don't know why. Maybe because mad is way more interesting than perfect. "For your information, Stevie Butts will ask anyone to sign his book. That Mercedes Lucia Mercada lady? He had her sign his book because he liked her name. That's all! She's not famous or anything. So there."

"I don't even care, okay? I don't want to be famous," she says, shoving the chair back under the table where it belongs. "I didn't even want to be stupid Cinderella! And for your information, a petit four is a dessert. I think what you meant to say was *petticoat*."

Then she stomps away. "Hey!" I yell. "I knew that! I knew that petit four is a dessert, and I meant to say that!" But she doesn't hear me.

"Places, everyone," says Mr. Mooney, and so everyone says their parts except me. I just watch from backstage. When it comes time for the fairy godmother, Mr. Mooney calls, "Fairy godmother?"

"Zoe's not here yet," says one of the stepsisters.

"Mary Margaret . . . could you?" Mr. Mooney calls.

I draggle myself onto the stage. When I dreamed about being in the play, there was never anything about playing other people's roles. "Winkle, twinkle, bobinkle," I say like I am bored, which I am. "If you don't get a move on, missy, you'll never make it to the party." Missy is what my mother calls me sometimes when she's a little put out with me. When she is feeling attached to me, she calls me Loverly.

Mr. Mooney gives me a look, because that is not exactly what the fairy godmother is supposed to say right then. "I know you know the right lines, Mary Margaret," he says. "Could you *please* just say them?"

It's true that I know all the lines. Zoe is late a lot, so I've been filling in for her. It's just that I get bored with all the same lines all the time. "But it doesn't even matter because there's no audience, and everyone knows their lines," I say. I still have my fighty feelings. They must be leftovers from arguing with Ellie.

"It does matter," Mr. Mooney says. "The last word of that line is supposed to be *ball*. The people who are working the spotlight are listening for that word. When they hear it, they know to put the spotlight on the gown. That's how we make the gown 'magically' appear. It's called a *cue*."

When he says the word *cue*, he says it like he's saying it to someone who isn't very smart. I look up to the lighting booth. "But there's no one up there running the spotlight right now. See?"

Mr. Mooney doesn't look. He just lifts up his glasses and rubs his eyes. This is something he does quite a bit when he talks at play practice. Mostly when he is talking to me. Then he looks at his watch. "We've all been working very hard," he says. "Let's quit early today."

This is fine with me. Because my day has not been that good. But then three things happen to change all that. The first thing is that Claire walks by and slides a note into my back pocket. "For JT," she whispers before she trots away. I open it, which is not really snooping since if it's a code note, I won't be able to read it, anyway. It is a code note, but, lucky for me, it has a big fat clue in it—something that looks like an e-mail address, because it has this in it: @. So I think I might be able to figure out the code from that.

The second thing is that Mr. Mooney tells us all as we are leaving that Miss Davis's snake died. "He passed away peacefully," he says. "But Miss Davis doesn't want us to use his picture in the calendar. She said she was very sorry, but it would be just too hard for her. The calendar needs to be finished by tomorrow, and we need a replacement."

Lucky for him, I have the perfect replacement. I tell him so, and he blasts a smile on me so bright that it almost knocks me right over. And even if it did, I wouldn't have cared.

And then the luckiest thing of all happens—the thing that is going to guarantee that I'll be Mr. Mooney's star for good. Baby Liza gets sick.

"Wash your hands!" my mother says. She says this a lot, even when no one is sick. JT says that she's a member of the G.E.P. That's short for Germ Extermination Patrol. He says it's a secret group that wants to make germs extinct, like the dinosaurs.

"I just did a few minutes ago," I say. I peel the wrapping off a piece of string cheese.

"Stop! Halt! Cease and desist!" my mother says, grabbing the cheese out of my hands to make sure that I do all those things. "You've been holding Liza. Her germs are all over your hands!"

"So?" I say. At our house, being sick = getting to stay home from school + watching all the TV you want. Plus I still haven't figured out how to be Cinderella, and if I can't be Cinderella, it doesn't really matter if I get sick.

"Well, you may not care, but other people do. If you don't wash your hands, you can infect other people."

Usually when I get an idea, it's because two things smash into each other in my brain. But this time the idea drops into my brain like a pebble into a pond. *Plink!* The idea is this: I am going to let Liza's germs hitch a ride on me all the way to Ellie. The germs will make her sick. She will be too sick to be in the play. And I will be Cinderella! But there is one thing I still need to know from my mom.

"How do they do that? Like would they make someone sick if I just touched that person?"

"They might. If you held Dad's hand and then he rubbed his eyes, the germs would get into his body through his eyes."

Huh! I think, very happy with myself because now I have a plan. "Okay," I say to my mother. "I will wash my hands."

"With soap. And wash them until you're done singing 'Happy Birthday' to yourself."

"Yes," I say, feeling very cooperative. "Yes, I will sing the birthday song so all the germs get washed off." Because I do not need Liza's germs right now. I won't need them until tomorrow morning before I leave for school.

I go into the bathroom and sing very quietly,

Happy Birthday to me
I don't like you, Ellie
You stole Mr. Mooney
Now you'll be sorry!

Then I sing, "Cha-cha-cha!"

The next morning, I hold my hand in front of Liza's mouth so that she'll breathe her germs on me. She goes kind of cross-eyed when she tries to focus on my hand. Then she flings her arms out, like she wants to touch my hands, but she can't get her arms to cooperate. It's a good thing that Mom and Dad love her no matter what, because she is not that good at anything. And she's goofy-looking. I stand there for a minute and let her germs soak in. But then I get worried that those breathing germs won't be enough to get Ellie sick, so I wipe Liza's nose with a Kleenex. But I'm not sure that will work, either, because there is a Kleenex between me and the germs. I need to make sure Liza's germs will stick to me until I can get them to Ellie.

I watch Liza while I think. She's still jerking her arms around. Finally she gets a fist near her mouth. Then I get an even better idea. I could wipe Liza's nose *with my hand.* At first I kick that idea right out of my head, because it's gross. But then I think about how much I want to be Cinderella. And I remember how my dad tells JT that if you work hard enough for what you want, then you'll get it. So wiping Liza's nose with my hand would be like working really hard for what I want. So then I have a little talk with myself that goes like this: Be brave! You can do it! I close my eyes and quick-wipe her nose with my hand. Liza's snot is slippery and slimy, but it dries pretty fast, and now I know that the germs will stick.

All the way to the bus stop and all the way to school on the bus, I hold my arms up, kind of like our minister when he says, "Praise the Lord!" only not up over my head. I hold them that way because I don't want to touch anyone or anything besides Ellie because I don't want to waste Liza's germs.

"What's wrong with your hands?" asks Stevie Butts when he gets on the bus.

"Nothing," I say. I slide over so he can sit down, but I keep my elbows propped against my body so my hands don't touch anything.

"Why are you holding them funny?"

I don't want to tell him what I'm doing. He won't understand. He's one of those Ellie-lovers. "I'm, uhhhh, just taking care of them," I say. And then I start talking very fast, which is what I do when I get nervous. "I think people aren't nice enough to their hands. Look at all our hands do for us. They snap, and they clap. Because of hands, we can thumb wrestle. And wear rings. And point at things. What if we had to use our elbows to point at things?" I keep my arm crooked and use my elbow to point out the window. "Look at that!" I yell.

"What? What?" says Stevie Butts.

"*That!*" I say, jabbing my elbow.

"The Beetle car or the mini-mall?" he asks. But by then, we have gone by both of them.

"See?" I say. "That's what I'm talking about. That's the kind of thing that would happen if we didn't have hands."

"I never really thought about that, but I guess you're right," he says. "Without hands, how would I hold the glass slipper while the prince and I are going around the kingdom looking for Cinderella?"

"Right!" I say.

Then his shoulders kind of droop. "I dropped the slipper three times yesterday at practice," he says. "I was awful."

"Rehearsal," I say. "And don't worry. You'll get better."

"Swear it? Because you're the one who said I should be in the play, Mary Margaret. I get laughed at already because of my name. I don't want to be laughed at because I mess up."

"I swear it," I say. Because how hard can it be to say two lines and hold on to a slipper?

"Maybe you could help me practice."

"Help you practice *holding* something?"

"Yeah. Because maybe I'm doing it wrong."

"Just hold on to it a little tighter."

Stevie Butts nods very serious. "Yeah, okay," he says. He closes his fist tight like he's gripping a sword. "I can do that."

Ellie hasn't been very friendly ever since we had that fight about JT's code. Until now, that has been okay with me. But in order for my plan to work, we need to get friendly—fast. Because I don't think germs stay good forever. They probably go stale about as fast as a piece of bubblegum. So when I get to school, I run fast like a rabbit, quick like a bunny over to the door where Ellie always waits. Everyone else always plays on the monkey bars and stuff, but not Ellie. She probably doesn't want to get her white shoes stomped on.

When I get close to her, I let my arms hang normal. I don't want to look suspicious. "Hi, Ellie," I say.

"Hi," she says. She looks at me for a second but then looks away fast.

I hold out my hands, germy side up. "I know a new dance," I say. "Want me to teach you?"

She crosses her arms. "No, thanks."

That's when I figure something out. If I want Ellie and me to be close, I am going to have to do what my mom and dad call "kiss and make up." That is what happens after they have a fight. And mostly what it means is that they say "Sorry," which I am not that good at doing. But I already have the germs on my hand, so I take a deep breath, and I say, "I am sorry . . ." and then I stop because what am I really sorry about? And the answer to that question is there's nothing I'm really sorry about.

But I don't even have to finish the "I'm sorry" sentence because Ellie throws her arms around me and says, "Me, too! I'm sorry, too! Let's not fight. Rehearsals have been dreadful while we were mad at each other. Show me the dance!"

I wish she would stop being so nice, because there is a little blip that goes off inside me that makes it hard to finish the plan. But the germs are ready to go, and the blip doesn't last. So I make up this dance where we have to hold hands through the whole thing. It is a very silly dance, and we step on each other's toes and bonk our heads together because she doesn't know the dance, and neither do I, even though I'm pretending to. Pretty soon we can't stop laughing. Ellie is laughing so hard that she is crying, and I bet in another minute she's going to wipe her tears away with one of her freshly germed hands. I feel that blip again. I kind of want her to get sick, but I kind of don't, and the "do" side of me is fighting with the "don't" side. But before either of them wins, she starts to put her hand up to her eye and then stops.

"I almost forgot," she says, reaching into her pocket and pulling out a little package. "Hand sanitizer," she says, "because it's flu season." I watch her put the gel on her hands and rub her hands together like she's erasing all the germs—and my best chance at getting to be Cinderella.

And then the bell rings, and it is time to go inside, and as we are walking in beside each other, she grabs my hand again, so that is how my number-one enemy and me end up walking down the hall together holding hands.

All day Ellie treats me like we're best friends. That works out good for me because it gives me more chances to give her Liza's germs. The germs probably wear out after a few hours, but I keep trying because you never know. They could still be good.

After school at play practice, I sit in the wings. I don't

follow Ellie around anymore on stage. I know what Cinderella is supposed to say—kind of—and where Cinderella is supposed to stand—sort of. To tell the truth, I'm bored. Opening night is next week, and unless Ellie gets sick or a bad case of stage fright, I won't be onstage anyway. I only half listen to what's going on. Mostly I work some more on breaking JT's code. The @ sign didn't turn out to be a good clue, after all. All I could figure out was that the note had someone's e-mail address in it. Big deal. I hate it that Claire broke the code a long time ago. I feel like a little kid who's easy to trick. I wonder if they are laughing at me. They haven't used me as their letter carrier since that last note that I gave JT from Claire, so maybe they know I looked at their notes. And even though JT is at play practice sometimes now because Mr. Mooney needed someone to run the spotlight and JT volunteered, I never see him and Claire talking. Maybe he doesn't like her after all. That would be a happiness.

"Zoe!" Mr. Mooney calls. "You're on!"

"She's not here yet," I grumble.

"Could you—?" he asks.

"Sure," I say. Without looking up from my paper, I yank my arm up and down in Ellie's/Cinderella's direction and say,

Fiddilly, Diddilly, Dee
It's time for you and me
To find the big party

Mr. Mooney doesn't say anything. He just spins his hand, which is a signal to the other actors to keep the scene going. I think he has given up on me ever saying those lines right.

After practice is finished, Ellie comes to find me.

"What are you doing?"

"Working on that code."

"Oh. You know, I thought about it some more after we fought," she says. "Maybe we could figure out what just one of the words is and then use that to figure out the rest."

"But which word?"

"Simple ones. One- or two- or three-letter words."

Ellie looks over my shoulder at my piece of paper. Before I washed the first note off my hand, I had copied it onto that paper. Then I had copied Claire's note back to JT onto the same piece of paper. I thought having them both in the same place might help me figure it out. The paper is getting pretty raggedy from my folding and unfolding it so many times, but we can still see the words.

"Here's a two-letter word," says Ellie. "Right at the end of the first note. It could be *do* or *my*."

"Or *is*," I say. "Or *on* or *in*. Or it could be *or*."

We puzzle about that for a while, but it seems like none of them work, except maybe *do* or *in* would come at the end of a sentence.

"What could the note be about?" she asks.

"That's what I'm trying to figure out," I snip at her.

"But can't you guess?"

I forget that I wasn't going to tell Ellie who wrote the note. "Yeah, it probably says something stupid like 'Dear Claire, I heart you forever and ever.' And then I make big smoochy, sloppy kissing noises. Ellie laughs. This makes me think that maybe she won't care that I read a note I wasn't supposed to. I take a chance and tell her about how the notes are from JT to Claire and from Claire to JT.

"Why do they write in code?" she asks.

"It might be because I'm famous in my family for being curious," I say.

"Oh," she says. "Having a brother sounds like fun."

"It does?" I ask. Because ever since JT and Claire started this stupid letter club, having a brother hasn't been that great.

Ellie nods. "It's boring at my house. Just me and my parents. And my mom never leaves me alone. She's always hanging over me, telling me how to do things before I even have a chance to try. She calls it 'helping' me. So I never have a chance to do anything like snoop."

"Really?" My mom is busy with Liza all the time, or she's working, so I have lots of chances to snoop. It's kind of like Ellie has too much mom, and I don't have enough.

"Do you really think JT likes her?" she asks.

I make more smooching noises, and she laughs. But talking about who the notes are to and from gives me an idea. "It's . . . JT!" I say.

Ellie looks around. "Where?"

"No, not the real JT. The last two letters of his note are his name." I point to the NX. "Now I can figure out the rest."

"You mean all the rest of the *N*'s and *X*'s," Ellie says. "But what about the others?"

"No, not just all the *J*'s and *T*'s. Remember how you said that sometimes a code alphabet is off by one letter? Maybe their code alphabet is off by a different number of letters. Now that we know *J* and *T*, we can figure out how many."

We try it by two letters, but that doesn't work. Then we try it by three letters, then four, and finally we can read the notes perfectly.

So the first note, HS CSY PMOI TYDDPIW? —NX, means *Do you like puzzles? —JT.*

And in the note that Claire wrote back, CIW, FYX QEMP FC QQ MW XSS WPSA. MQ QI? GPEVMRIX@ EGGIWW.KIX means *Yes, but mail by MM is too slow. IM me? clarinet@access.net.*

"That's all?" I ask. "Just a couple of stupid sentences about whether or not they both like codes?" I scrunch up the piece of paper and throw it across the room.

"Why are you mad?" Ellie asks.

"Because when something is in code, you think it must be really important. Otherwise why put it in code at all?"

"Then why did JT do it?"

"To annoy me," I say. "To keep me out and let Claire in."

"But he didn't even know you were going to read them," she says.

"I told you I was famous in my family," I say. I feel all flat. If there had been something interesting or important in those notes, then I could get why JT wrote in code. But now it really does feel like the whole thing was a big trap JT built for me. Like he was saying to Claire, "Watch what I can get my little sister to do."

"That was really smart," Ellie says.

"What?"

"The way you figured out the code."

Her saying that puts a little gust of life into me. "Thanks," I say. "I thought you'd figure it out before me."

"Why?"

"Because you're, you know, pretty good at everything."

"Oh, that. I don't want to be," she says, "but I feel like I have to be that way. That's why I really wanted the role of the wicked stepsister."

"Wait. You wanted to be the *wicked stepsister*?"

"Yes. At the beginning I didn't want to be Cinderella at all. I wanted to play somebody who was really awful. I cried when I found out that I had been cast as Cinderella. But even though it's not who I really wanted to be at first, I like playing Cinderella now."

"Why didn't you tell Mr. Mooney right away that you didn't want to be Cinderella?"

"I don't know. Because he'd already decided what he wanted me to be, and I'm not supposed to contradict adults, and in a way, if I said I didn't want to be what he wanted me to be, that's contradicting him."

"Why did you want to be a stepsister? That's a lot smaller of a part."

Ellie crosses her arms on the table and lays her chin on them. "I'm tired of being all good, when inside that's not always the way I feel. Sometimes I just want to scream and yell. Sometimes I even want to push and shove or grab a toy back instead of sharing."

"Then why don't you sometimes do that stuff?"

"Because my mother always says nobody likes mean girls. The reason I wanted to be a stepsister was because then I could be mean, and no one would ever know that it was *me* who was being mean. They would just think it was the evil stepsister."

"People would still like you, I bet. You're the only one in our class who *doesn't* do stuff like that sometimes."

"So you'd still like me?"

I shrug. "Sure, as much as I did before," I say. Then I think, And maybe even more. Because when you didn't like someone to begin with because she's perfect, and then you find out she isn't perfect and doesn't even want to be, liking her more is the only thing that's left.

At dinner, I don't say anything. JT is very talky. He talks about how many people have bought *his* calendars (when they are really *my* calendars). About how Mr. Mooney (*my* teacher) told JT he was a fast learner on the spotlight. I notice that he does not say anything about Claire. He never says anything about Claire. This makes me think JT probably doesn't want Mom and Dad to know about her.

I don't get what is up with JT and me. I helped him out by passing those notes between him and Claire—notes that I couldn't read. I thought JT was kind of trusting me, and that felt good. But JT + code = he still thinks I'm a sneak. And when I figured out the code and saw that the notes didn't even say anything big, it made everything even worse. It's like JT and Claire have a club and a clubhouse. They won't let me join the club, but they make me watch them having fun through the clubhouse window. I feel left out. And now that JT is talking about Mr. Mooney *loving* him, I also feel mean. I want to get back at JT, and suddenly I know just how I'll do it.

"JT has a girlfriend," I blurt out, interrupting JT right in the middle of a sentence.

JT's face turns bright red. "I do not," he says, kicking me under the table. Mom and Dad are looking at me, all curious. I can tell that this is a current event for them.

"She's the only reason that he's helping with the spotlight. Her name is Claire. She's in the play. They pass notes back and forth," I say. Inside I am thinking, Nan-ah, nan-ah, boo-boo.

"We do not!" he says.

"Maybe not anymore. Not now that you know clarinet @access.net."

He squinches up his eyes at me. "How would you know, Mary You'll-Regret-This?"

I gulp then, because I realize that the only way I would know her e-mail address was if I read the notes. Private notes. That were in code. "You still just can't control yourself, can you?" says JT. "You still have to know everything. You can't just stay out of my life!"

"I would, but your life keeps crashing into mine!" I say. "*I'm* the one who wanted to be in the play, remember?"

"Yeah, and *you're* the one who dragged me into it— remember that?" JT stands up. "I was the one who was helping you. And you wonder why I call you annoying."

"I'm not annoying! I'm naturally curious," I say.

"Save it for someone who cares," he says. And then he goes to his room.

My parents are both staring at me. "You know how he feels about his privacy," my dad says.

"It was his own fault," I say. "He asked me to give a note to Claire. I held on to it all day without looking at it, but then I couldn't find Claire, and the note kept poking me. It was hurting me. What could I do?"

"Mary Margaret," says my mom, "I expect more from you."

"I know!" I say. "I get it!"

"I think you know what to do," my dad says. "Don't worry. He hasn't bitten anyone recently." My dad is trying to be funny, but it doesn't work that well with me right now.

I trudge up the stairs to JT's room. All the way there, I am thinking about how my mom expects more from me, and I don't know why she does. Can't she see that I'm doing my best? Can't she see that I was able to hold back my natural curiosity a lot longer this time than ever before? Things would go a lot better for me if everyone would stop "expecting more" from me.

When I knock, JT opens his door, but he won't let me in. "What?" he says.

I sigh and look straight up at the ceiling. "I'm sorry for reading your dumb old notes," I say. Talking to the ceiling is easier than talking to JT when he doesn't like me.

"Let me guess. Dad made you come up."

"So?" I say.

"So you're just doing this because Dad said. You're never sorry about anything. Maybe you can't be. Maybe you were born with some kind of defect." He sticks the back of his wrist to his forehead and waggles his fingers at me, pretending that's what I look like.

I reach for him, but he backs up and slams the door in my face. "I don't have any defect!" I yell through the door. "I can too be sorry!" To prove it, I tell him all the things that make me sorry. I pound on the door between each thing. "I'm sorry that we had meat loaf for dinner"—*pound*—"and that you have a bigger room than I do"—*pound*—"and that I can't be Cinderella"—*pound*—"and I'm *really* sorry that I had to come up here and apologize to you!" What I don't say is what I just figured out—that I really am sorry about reading the notes because it means that JT doesn't like me anymore. I guess all that pounding on JT's door pounds the tears right out of me. I lean my cheek against the "GO THE DISTANCE—RUN CROSS-COUNTRY" bumper sticker he has on his door and start to cry.

"That's what I mean," JT says through the door. "You're just feeling sorry for yourself!"

That makes me cry even harder. JT opens the door slowly and pulls me into his room. "Cut it out," he says, but nicely.

He pulls over the desk chair so I can sit down, then

hands me a Kleenex so I can mop up my face. When I'm done, he gives me a piece of licorice. It's old, but still— he gave it to me, so that's an almost-happiness. "Why are you being nice to me now when you were just being so mean?" I ask.

"I don't know. Because all that water from your crying was going to ruin the stuff on my door. Besides, Mom and Dad would kill me if they think I made you cry. And anyway, that whole note idea was probably pretty dumb."

"Yeah, you should apologize to me for laughing at me."

"What? I wasn't laughing at you."

"You put the note in code so you and Claire could laugh at me."

"I wasn't even thinking about you when I put the note in code."

"Then why did you do it?"

"I wanted to get to know Claire, but I feel funny just talking to girls. I thought this would be a way to kind of see if . . . you know, she was interested."

"You were making eyes at her? In code?" I ask. Making eyes is what my mother calls it when a boy and a girl like each other in a special way but still think it's icky to hold hands.

"I know it's different," he says, "but it worked. Remember that first day that we met her when we were arguing in the lobby, with Liza? Claire came in carrying a bunch of books. And one of them was on crossword puzzles. So I guessed that she likes word games."

"So you didn't do all that to trap me?"

"You might not believe it, but I have got way better things to do with my time than think up new ways to trick you. In a way, though, I owe you. If you hadn't dragged me into the play, I wouldn't have met her. And now Claire and I have the play to talk about—and you."

"That's what I mean—you're laughing about me."

"No, Claire thinks you're really good. She thinks Mr. Mooney should lighten up a little." He grins goofy again. "And I think you're even more dramatic offstage than on." He puts his hands together and puts them up to his chin, then flutters his eyelashes. *"Oh, poor me!"* he says, making his voice all high. *"My life is so awful! I have to sweep the hearth, and no one loves me!"*

"Ha ha," I say. "Very funny. You'd be more helpful if you had a wand you could turn me into Cinderella with."

"Sorry. The only thing I can wave over you is the spotlight."

This gives me an idea. "Hey! Maybe you and me could work out a code—just in case Ellie gets stage fright."

"She's not going to get stage fright," JT says. "And even if she did, what would we need a code for?"

"To give me time to get ready to go onstage."

JT flicks at my pigtail. "Come on, Mary Margaret. What are the chances?"

"I know it is extremely unlikely," I say, "but couldn't we do it, just in case? You said that you owe me. You did a code with Claire, and now I want a code-thingy that's between just you and me."

JT groans. "Okay. You want a signal."

And then we work out a secret signal so that I can let him know if I do get to be Cinderella at the very last minute, which I probably won't. But "probably won't" is a lot like "extremely unlikely." Neither of them means "It will never happen." Which could be good news for me.

12. Cue Mary Marguerite!
My Time to Shine

I asked nicely. I begged loudly. I even tried to bribe my mother into leaving Liza home on opening night. "I'll watch her while you take a nap every day for a month," I say. "If you'll get a babysitter."

"It's tempting," my mom says. "But it would be silly to hire a sitter when Liza is going to sleep through the whole thing anyway. She still has a little bit of a cold, so I hate to leave her. And she's always done with her fussy time by seven-thirty or so."

"It's the *or so* that's the problem," I say. There have been lots of times that Liza has still been awake and cranky after I've gone to bed at 8:30. "I don't want my little sister ruining the play!"

"If she's fussy, I'll just take her out for a few minutes and feed her. After your father takes you and JT over early—"

"And Hershey," I say.

"Hershey?" she asks.

"We needed a footman—well, actually, an animal that

would turn into a footman—so I volunteered Hershey," I say. It didn't happen exactly that way. What happened was that I begged Mr. Mooney that if I couldn't be in the play then at least could my rabbit be in the play—please, please, *please*. And he asked if I planned on having my rabbit remain securely in its cage, and if it somehow didn't remain in its cage, would I take full responsibility for it. I said sure. Then Mr. Mooney was quiet while he lifted up his glasses and rubbed his eyes, so I said one more *please* and tried to make my eyes big and sad. And he said okay, and he hoped he wouldn't regret it.

"Well, then, after your father takes you and JT and Hershey over early, he'll come back and pick up the rest of the family." My mom kisses me on the top of my head as she walks by. This means that the conversation is over. As usual, I am stuck with Liza. That's what's weird about brothers and sisters and parents. I didn't get to pick them, like I got to pick Hershey. I just ended up with them. Like I end up with cards I don't want when I'm playing Old Maid.

But it's different from playing Old Maid, too. Because in Old Maid, even if you get the Old Maid, there's always the chance that someone else will pick her from your hand, but in a family you're stuck with whoever you get. Sometimes that works out okay. I like the parents I got. It's a good thing I didn't get Ellie's mom because I mostly do things wrong before I get them right, so if I had gotten Ellie's mom, me and her probably would have had a lot of bad days. I also got lucky with JT, who is usually nice and mostly useful. But then my luck changed when Liza came. She is only sometimes nice, and she isn't useful at all, and she's always stinking up the place with her dirty diapers. She's definitely the Old Maid in our family. So sometimes the sorting out doesn't work out. And mostly you can't tell ahead of time when it will work out and when it won't. In a family you get what you get, and then you're stuck with those people forever.

Fortunately, you can change almost everything else lots of times. On the day that we're going to put on the play for the very first time, I spend a lot of time getting ready to be in the spotlight. I take a shower and even comb out all of my hair afterward. Usually I only comb out the top layer because the bottom part is too snarly, and it hurts to comb it out, so I just leave it alone. But this time I just keep yanking the comb through the snarls, even though it hurts, because this is a special occasion. Then my mom dries it for me with the blow-dryer.

"Do you want me to curl it?" she asks.

"Curls are too springy," I say. "Can you do teeny braids all over my head instead?"

"I'm not sure they had braids back in Cinderella's time," my mom says. I think my mom has forgotten how smart I am, so I remind her. "Cinderella didn't have a time," I say. "It's a fairy tale."

"Oh, Loverly," she says, "it's just that teeny braids are not very Cinderella-ish."

"They are my kind of Cinderella-ish, and since it is extremely unlikely that I will get to play Cinderella, it doesn't matter."

My mom waggles her head like she can't believe me, but then she starts braiding. She braids for a long, long time, and I don't squirm at all. When she's finished, she helps me put on blush and mascara. And when I finally look in the mirror, I look so zippy-tastic that I think Mr. Mooney will take one look at me and tell Ellie to take a seat in the wings because Mary Margue*rite* has arrived.

Or maybe he won't have to tell her that. Because maybe she's sick. I call Ellie to find out. "Thanks for asking how I'm feeling," she says. "I'm excited and a little nervous."

"So you're not feeling sickish or anything?"

"No. My stomach feels funny, but my mom says it's just nerves." She sniffs, which is almost like a sniffle. This fills me up with hope.

"Is that your nose running?" I ask.

"What? Oh, no. I was sniffing because it smells good in here. My mom just baked brownies."

"Oh," I say. Some of the hope floats out of me.

Then I hear her say, "Ouch! Mom, I just combed it. What? Okay. Just a minute, and I'll be right there." She starts talking to me again. "Sorry," she says. "I think my mom is more nervous than I am."

"About what?"

"Right now about my curtsy. A few minutes ago it

was about my dancing. She's been teaching me to waltz."

"But your prince doesn't even know how to waltz." Cameron is a sixth-grader, but he hasn't grown into his feet yet. His feet are ninth-graders. Maybe even tenth-graders.

"I know, but it's easier to let her teach me than to try to explain that. Besides, if I told her about Cameron, she'd drag him into the lessons, too. And then he'd hate me, and everyone would be able to tell that the prince actually hates Cinderella. That would be bad for the play. It's just better if I go along with my mom."

"So . . . no tickle of a sore throat or anything?" I feel a little bad that I slimed her, but I still hope Liza's germs haven't given up. I know I shouldn't, but I can't help it.

"No," she says. Then I hear her whisper something else to her mother. "They're fine. Just leave them . . . no one really cares about what color of nail polish I have on." She says to me, "I have to go, Mary Margaret. See you in a little while."

When it's almost time to leave for the play, I get Hershey from her cage and put her into Itzy's crate. Andy showed me twice how to latch the cage. He wanted me to show him that I knew how to do it, but I just said, "All right!" because closing a cage isn't that hard to do. And because, except for looking like a real movie star, I wasn't having that good of a day, so I wasn't in the mood to listen to him.

After Dad drops off me and JT and Hershey, JT helps

me get Hershey to the right place onstage. She's hunched at the back of her cage, and her whiskers are going *twitch-twitch-twitch*. I tell her not to worry. She's going to be great.

"Psssst! Don't forget about the signal," I say to him as he's leaving.

JT points across the stage. "Ellie is right there, and she's fine. We're not going to need the signal, Mary Margaret."

Can't he see I'm Mary Marguer*ite*? "Tell me you remember, though."

JT is suddenly standing in the spotlight, and I hear a laugh. Claire's laugh. "Hi, JT," she says from way up in the spotlight booth. He smiles and takes a bow.

"Hey! No fooling around with the spotlight!" yells Mr. Mooney. The spotlight goes off, and Claire laughs again.

I pull on JT's arm to remind him that I'm there. "Just in case, JT. Tell me you remember just in case."

"Yeah, sure, I remember, Mary Don't-You-Fret."

"Very funny," I say. But he is already walking offstage.

After a while, it gets wild backstage. Everyone is talking louder and faster than usual and racing around looking for stuff. "I can't find the glass slipper," says Stevie Butts. "I know I had it before I went into the bathroom."

"Then check the bathroom," I tell him. "Maybe you set it down in there."

"Has anyone seen my crown?" yells Cameron.

"Has anyone seen *Zoe*?" shouts Mr. Mooney.

"She'll be here," says Wicked Stepsister #2. "I just talked to her an hour ago."

I cut through the prop section to where the costumes are. Ellie's there, in her Cinderella hearth dress. She doesn't look sick or even very nervous, which is why my heart shrinks up, and my feet stop. Because right then it finally sinks in that Ellie is going to be Cinderella, and I am not. I stand behind a rack of props. There's a space between Cinderella's crown and the fairy godmother's hat, and I watch everyone through it. Lots of kids buzz around Ellie, like worker bees around the queen bee. Mostly they are saying, "Break a leg, Ellie." That's code for "good luck" except it's not that good a code because everybody knows it. Every time someone says that to her or tells her how great she looks, it feels like someone is sticking me with a pin. *Ooo! Ouch! Stop that!* Because it should be me standing there in the middle of all the happiness. It should be me wearing the hearth dress, ready to say my lines. I had the idea for the calendar. I even got a real celebrity for the calendar. And then, even after I didn't get the part, I made a plan for how I could still be Cinderella.

But my plan didn't work. Now watching everyone light up Ellie is what my mother would call "more than I can stand." I never liked being Cindy Two during practices, but I got used to it. It's like getting a shot. I know it's going to hurt, but I know from all the other shots I've had how much it will hurt and how long the hurt will last. After I went to a few play practices, I knew what play practice would be like and how it would feel to watch Ellie practicing to be Cinderella. But I didn't know that tonight would feel different. I didn't know that tonight would be like getting a hundred shots, one right after the other.

And then Mr. Mooney comes over. "Good, good," he says, clapping his hands to get everyone's attention off of Ellie. "Everyone's in their costumes. Steven, I see you found the slipper. Anyone nervous? That's normal. Just remember, you've practiced hard. You know your lines. Now everyone just relax and have fun. And remember— *slower* and *louder*. You can never speak too slowly or too loudly."

Everyone walks away, jabbering to one another, except Mr. Mooney and Ellie. And even though I'm standing right there, *right in front of them* except for that rack of props between us, they don't see me. He sticks out his hand to her. "Ready?" he says.

"Ready," she says, putting her hand in his. And then they do a silly handshake that they both know and I don't. A handshake that ends with him beaming his smile down on her. And I know smiles can't really talk, but it's like this one does. It says, "You are the starriest of stars, the favoritest of all my favorite students."

Blecch, I think. *Pitooey*. If I'm not going to get to be Cinderella, I wish I could go home. But my parents are coming, so I'm stuck here. That doesn't mean I have to watch. When I turn to leave, though, my elbow bumps against the rack, and everything on it rattles and a candlestick crashes over.

"Mary Margaret!" Ellie says, all happy. It's easy for her to be all happy. She gets to be Cinderella.

"Cindy Two!" Mr. Mooney says, waving his clipboard at me. "Happy Opening Night!"

"Just call me Mary Margaret," I say, all glum.

But he doesn't hear me because right then he says, "Eight minutes until curtain time. Eight minutes, people."

Ellie runs over and throws her arms around me. "Isn't it exciting?" My body goes all hard and straight like an icicle. But before I can answer, Ellie's mother comes over.

Ellie quits the hugging, which is good for me. "Did I forget something?" she asks her mom. "I double-checked to make sure I had everything, but maybe I left—"

"No, you didn't forget anything—well, you did forget to turn off the light in your room, but that's not such a big deal," Ellie's mom says. But it seems to me like it is a big deal to Ellie's mom, because then she says, "I've told you again and again, but I guess it's just something we'll have to keep working on."

"Oh, sorry!" Ellie says, all serious. "I was just so excited . . ."

"I know. And I wanted to come back and tell you good luck. Don't forget—shoulders back, chin up, and don't let your voice peter out at the end of your lines. I've noticed that you've started doing that, especially in Act Three, and that's really your moment to shine, isn't it?"

Ellie doesn't say anything.

"I'm sure you'll do it right," her mother says. "You know what I always say. If you can't do a job right . . ."

". . . don't do it at all," Ellie says. Her voice slouches when she says it.

"That's right," says her mother. "Make us proud, darling."

After her mother leaves, Ellie looks wilty, like a plant that gets too much sun and no water. She starts walking back and forth between the prop rack and the costume area. "I wish she wouldn't do that," Ellie says to the floor.

"Doesn't she know she's supposed to say 'break a leg' instead of 'good luck'?"

"Not that," Ellie says. "I don't care about that."

I don't have time to find out what she means, though, because just then Mr. Mooney whispers, "Places, everyone!"

This is it! The play is going to begin.

When Ellie looks up, she looks kind of like Hershey looked in her cage when I put her onstage. She looks all hunched up on herself. And she's breathing funny—she's panting like Itzy does when Andy and I run around in the yard with him.

Ellie grabs my arms. Here we go again, I think. More hugging. But then she says, "I can't do it."

For a minute I forget that this is exactly what I have been hoping for, and I start to argue with her. "What do you mean you can't do it?"

"I'll ruin it." She's talking like a robot. "I can't do it. I can't do it. I'll make a mistake. I'll ruin it."

"Ruining it is my little sister's job," I say.

The lighting backstage is very dim. I can see Mr. Mooney from across the stage, but I can tell he doesn't see what's happening with Ellie.

And then I remember that this is what I wanted—Ellie out of the way so I could be on center stage, right where I know in my heart I belong. My heart is leaping and jumping around inside of me, bouncing off the walls of my rib cage. I am going to be Cinderella! Me! Mary Marguer*ite!* Onstage. In the spotlight. And at the end everyone is going to stand up and clap, and I am going to take a huge bow, and afterward Mr. Mooney is going to say that I saved the show, and it will be true.

I pull Ellie behind the castle set where no one can see us. She stands there like she's frozen. "Put your arms up," I hiss. "I need the dress!"

"I never should have tried out for this stupid play," she whispers through the dress as I try to pull it over her head.

"It's stuck!" I whisper. "Help me!"

I hear Mr. Mooney whisper, "Stepmother, cue the spotlight," on the other side of the stage.

I forgot about the spotlight! When the stepmother calls *"Cin-der-el-la!"* from offstage, that's JT's cue to turn the spotlight on, and then the stepmother is supposed to run into the spotlight and call for her again and then run off-stage. And then the curtain is supposed to go up, and the spotlight will be right on Cinderella. And all that would happen, except that JT and me worked out a special signal. I do two fake sneezes—big, LOUD sneezes. So even though the stepmother is still going to call *"Cin-der-el-la,"* the spotlight will not come on. At least that is the plan. I hope JT is paying attention to my sneezes instead of paying attention to Claire.

I give the dress another hard yank, and it's like trying to pull a dress off a rag doll. Each time I yank the dress, Ellie seems to come with it because she's so floppy.

Then it gets even harder to get the dress off because Ellie's shoulders start to shake. "I'm never going to be good enough for her," Ellie says.

"For who?"

"My mother. There's always a light I left on or a curtsy I messed up."

"Uh-huh," I say, because I am kind of busy right then trying to get the dress off her and onto me so that I can be Cinderella.

"I'll never make her proud," she says.

"Sure you will," I say. "Just not tonight." But then I start to feel the way I do when I take a sip of hot chocolate when it's still too hot. I expect it to be all warm and sweet, but instead it burns my mouth, and then I can't taste anything. But I go ahead and drink it anyway because I keep expecting it will taste good.

"She isn't proud unless I do everything right. I'm just not good enough."

The dress is off of one of Ellie's arms, but it's stuck on the other, so it's kind of half on and half off. Under it, she's wearing a leotard. That's so that she will be able to change into Cinderella's ball gown quickly offstage instead of going all the way to the dressing room.

When I see that leotard, something happens inside me. It's like when I'm in our van, and it starts raining really hard so I can't see anything but the water pouring down over the windshield, but then Mom turns on the windshield wipers, and then I can see the road and other cars and everything outside of the van. When I see Ellie's leotard and remember that I am only wearing underwear, it's like windshield wipers inside of me come on. I see that Ellie is what my mom would call "prepared." She paid attention at practice. She rehearsed her lines until she got them just right. She even got a lot better at pronunciating. It's true what all those kids were saying right before the play. Ellie is a good Cinderella—a better Cinderella than I would be. And she shouldn't not be Cinderella just because she thinks that if she goofs up she'll wreck the whole play.

"*Cin-der-el-la!*" yells the stepmother from offstage. I can see her standing near Mr. Mooney. She is waiting for the spotlight to come on so she can run into it and yell *"Cin-der-el-la!"* again.

Please, JT, I think. Please, please remember that I sneezed twice, and don't turn on the spotlight yet. Just give me one more minute to get Ellie onstage.

I shove Ellie's arm back through the armhole, so the dress is back on her all the way.

"What are you doing?" she says.

Giving up on being Cinderella and saying good-bye to my dream, that's what I am doing. "Even if you make a mistake, you won't ruin the play," I say. "If you make a mistake, just keep going, just like Mr. Mooney said. You *can* do this. You have to do it." And once my mouth says it, my heart starts nodding like it agrees.

The only problem with all that is that Ellie doesn't agree. *"You* do it, Mary Margaret. I can't!" she says. "I keep thinking about what my mom said about doing it right and I—I—I just *can't* go out there."

Suddenly I have an idea. "Borrow my mom," I say. "My mom is used to mistakes. I make them all the time. She's happy if I just do my best."

"I can't do that—pretend to have a different mom!"

"If you can pretend to be Cinderella, then you can pretend to have a different mom."

"But I don't even know what your mom looks like!" she says.

I grab her arm and drag her up to the end of the curtain and pull it back a teeny bit. "There!" I whisper. "The one with the fussy baby. That's her."

"*Cin-der-el-la!*" yells the stepmother. The yell is louder this time, and it sounds a little nervous.

"She looks nice," says Ellie.

"She is. She used to be even better, but then she had a baby."

"I don't think—"

But there is no time for thinking, and if she doesn't get out there *right now*, I might change my mind. "Just go!" I say, and I spin her around so she's facing the stage.

The spotlight lights up the curtain. When the curtain opens, Ellie will be standing in it. Good-bye, Mary Marguerite, I think sadly as I give Ellie a little push onto center stage. Then the curtain comes up, and Ellie is in the spotlight. And that thing about borrowing my mom must have really worked, because it's like Ellie *is* Cinderella. She's doing everything just like she practiced it, and even though I know we're not, it really does seem like we're in a kingdom long, long ago and far, far away. A kingdom where everything happens just like it's supposed to.

Until a few things go ka-fluey.

Between Act One and Act Two is when it starts. Zoe is not here. Which means that Cinderella does not have a fairy godmother. Mr. Mooney looks at me over the top of his glasses and sighs like he wishes he did not have to say the words. "Cindy Two, can you play the fairy godmother?"

I think about this for a minute. If I can't be Cinderella, I don't want to be anybody. "Dream big." That's what grown-ups say, but then when I do dream big, things don't always work out that well. And playing the fairy god-mother feels like I'm admitting that I was wrong to think I could be Cinderella. It feels like I'm giving in or giving something up.

Mr. Mooney waves his arm at the stage. "I know you know the lines," he whispers. "Just think—you'll get to be the one who makes everyone's dreams come true."

Except my own, I think.

"And the show needs you."

There's part of me that still wants to say no, but the

show needs . . . Mary Margue*rite!* And that means Mr. Mooney needs *me.*

"Okay," I whisper. "But only if you promise me something."

"What's that?"

"Don't ever call me Cindy Two again. It makes me feel . . . squashed."

And even though it's almost time for the next act to start, Mr. Mooney stops right then. "I am sorry," he says. "I should have realized that."

"Yeah," I say. "I know." But now that I know he gets it, I don't want him to feel bad so I say, "I better get into the fairy godmother dress."

He gives me a big hug and says, "Thank you."

I think about how he didn't give me the part of Cinderella because he said he couldn't count on me to say the lines right. "Is this kind of like being able to count on me?" I ask him.

"Yes," he says, turning up his smile so bright that I feel like maybe I'm going to need sunglasses. "It most certainly is."

And that is how I end up in an itchy, poofy pink dress waving a wand around and making Cinderella's dreams come true. Even though I feel a little silly, I say the lines just the way the fairy godmother would, even the ones I think are dumb, and I even use the singsongy fairy godmother voice that Zoe used whenever she *did* make it to practice on time, which wasn't that often.

It feels good to be onstage, even if I am only the fairy godmother. At least sometimes all those people in the audience are looking at me—the times that they aren't all looking at Cinderella, anyway. I sneak a look at the audience. My mom and dad are both looking right at me, smiling. They look a little confused because I am the fairy godmother, but happy and proud. My dad gives me the "thumbs up" sign. I see Andy, too. His mouth is hanging open in a big O, so I guess he is surprised.

Being onstage also means that I get to be close to the action, and there is a lot of action. More action than there is supposed to be. But plays are kind of like that—you never know what's going to happen. Like Stevie Butts holds the slipper tighter, just like I told him to. But at the part where he shows the prince that he's found the slipper, he's holding on too tight. The prince (Cameron) is pulling and pulling, but that slipper seems stuck to Stevie Butts's hand—almost like he used Super Glue. But he wouldn't have done something dumb like that—*would he?*

I hear Cameron whisper "Let go!" at the same time that he tries to pull it out of Stevie Butts's hand, and finally Stevie Butts does let go, and the slipper flies out of his hand and over Cameron's head and crashes onto the floor. Fortunately, it's not really made of glass, so it doesn't break. The audience laughs, and Stevie Butts covers his face with his hands at first. Then he runs over and picks up the slipper and gives it to Cameron.

We have to change the set from the castle to Cinderella's house for the last scene, and everyone is scurrying around carrying props, so I'm not sure exactly how it happens, but Hershey gets loose. No one but me notices it until the prince is getting ready to try the slipper on the first stepsister's foot. But all of a sudden, there is Hershey, hopping out from under *that* stepsister's long dress. One by one, everyone onstage notices Hershey hop-hop-hopping across the stage.

So I start to go onstage to get Hershey because I had said yes when Mr. Mooney asked me if I would take full responsibility for Hershey. But when I walk by him, Mr. Mooney stops me. "You can't!" he says. "The fairy godmother isn't in this scene."

Hershey is hopping around faster and faster, like she's scared and doesn't know what to do. I think about what is supposed to come next—the end of the play is what's coming next. And at the end of a play, there is usually a lot of clapping. And Hershey does not like loud noises, so all that clapping will probably make her go freaky. And what if she jumps out into the audience and runs away? I can't just stand there when Hershey needs my help.

There's only one thing I can do. I invent a way for the fairy godmother to be in the scene. Which means that I have to add a few lines of my own. I kind of glide onto center stage, where Ellie is standing. The stepmother and sisters and prince and even Stevie Butts all freeze and then look toward where Mr. Mooney is standing offstage.

I know they are all wondering what the fairy godmother is doing there.

"Don't forget, Cinderella!" I say in my singsongy fairy godmother voice. "True love can come to anyone," which is a dumb thing to say, but it's what I think the godmother would have said if she had stopped by at just that part of the story. And then I make little kissing sounds, like I'm hinting that true love is coming to Cinderella, which it is. But those little kissing sounds also make Hershey hop right over to me. I scoop her up and disappear offstage, calling behind me, "All you have to do, dear, is believe. Be-leeeeee-ve!"

Some of the other kids onstage snicker, but mostly everyone is too surprised to say anything. And then Ellie does something she has never, ever done, probably in her life. She does something wrong on purpose. She puts both her hands to her heart and makes up a line. "Oh, Fairy Godmother," she says, "because of you, I do believe!" So the whole thing looks like it really is supposed to be part of the play instead of me making it up to catch my rabbit. Which is pretty great. The rest of the play goes just the way it's supposed to, and the glass slipper fits Cinderella, and she and the prince hold hands (ewww!) and make eyes at each other like they really are in love. And then Cinderella says the very last line of the play, "There's so much happiness in my heart!"

And I feel the very same way, because when each of us steps up to take a bow, the audience claps just as long and loud for me and Hershey, who I am still holding, as they do for Ellie. My mom with Liza, my dad with the video camera, and Andy with his tie that has gold stars on it—they are all smiling up at me and clapping, and so is everyone else, and it feels like I am in a glitter globe with glitter floating all around me. Mr. Mooney has tucked his clipboard under his arm, and he's clapping louder than anyone else. And *that* makes me feel like I'm a Christmas tree all strung with lights and someone has just plugged me in. So I guess I don't even have to be Cinderella to feel all a-twinkle. Which is a big surprise to Mary Marguerite. And to me.

HOLLYWOOD WALK OF FAME

After the play, all of us hang around and eat the "worms in mud" that I created that afternoon and brought to share. It's chocolate pudding with gummy worms and pretzels mixed in, but no one eats it that way. Mostly the kids just pick out the gummy worms, suck the pudding off, and then eat the worms. I might have to work a little more on that recipe.

I'm talking to Ellie and Mr. Mooney and some other kids when JT comes to find me. Claire is tagging along behind him. "So what happened?" he says.

"Yeah," says Claire. "You used the signal, so we were expecting you to show up onstage."

Now, thanks to Claire, everyone is looking at me. "What signal?" says Mr. Mooney.

Claire starts to blab everything that was between me and JT. "Mary Margaret thought—"

But then JT interrupts Claire before she can tell everyone I was so desperate to be Cinderella that I even worked out a signal. "She worked out a signal with me in case there was a problem backstage at the last minute," he says. "Two loud sneezes meant I should delay the spotlight."

"I never knew about that," says Mr. Mooney.

"I know," JT says. "It's just something that she and I worked out."

"It's a good thing they did," says Ellie. "Because I did have a problem." And then she explains about how she didn't want to go out onstage at the last minute. "It was Mary Margaret who changed my mind. She told me that of course I could do it and then pushed me out onto the stage. Once I was out there, I was fine."

"Fine?" says Claire. "You were great!"

"You were perfect," Mr. Mooney says.

Ellie's smile kind of straightens out right then. I remember what she said about not liking it when people call her perfect.

"Not *quite* perfect," I say. "She invented a few lines, remember?" And then everyone laughs because it was my fault that she had to do that. Ellie looks glad that I said it.

"So let me think about this, Mary Margaret," says Mr. Mooney. "You got Cinderella onstage, you played the fairy godmother, which wasn't even your part, and you rescued the play from your rabbit. So you saved the play *three* times?"

"Four, actually," I say. "The calendar, remember?"

"Of course!" says Mr. Mooney. "The calendar. You

came up with a last-minute replacement! The gubernatorial candidate."

Yeah, I think. Plus it was my idea to begin with. Plus I got Caleb Strong to say he'd be in our calendar when nobody thought he would. Plus— But then I stop adding. I don't like math much, anyway.

We do the play three more times, and I get to play the fairy godmother once more, because Zoe's soccer team is in a tournament that's on the same night as one of the performances. The other two times I help Mr. Mooney out backstage, and he only ever calls me Mary Margaret, not Cindy Two. He even lets Hershey back into the play, once Stevie Butts confesses that he's the one who let her out. He was mad at me because I was the one who told him he should be in the play, and then he messed up. "I wanted to get back at you," he told me. "I was sorry as soon as I let her out, and I tried to catch her, but then she hid under one of the stepsisters' dresses, and then the scene started." I told him it was okay, because it was. Hershey and I got to have a scene together, and that was pretty cool.

Ellie never needs me to push her out onto the stage again. She says that's because of everything that happened on that first night. When she gets nervous about not doing it exactly right, she remembers to borrow my mom. She thinks about how she made up some lines on opening night and remembers that they worked. "I liked doing it," she says to me one day at school a few weeks after the play is over. "I liked making up the lines."

"Don't tell Mr. Mooney that!" I say, packing down the clay on the volcano we're building. After closing night, Ellie and I asked if we could be desk buddies, and Mr. Mooney said okay. We think our volcano is going to be the best in the class. Ellie is very good about following the rules, so she's in charge of making sure the volcano actually works. I am very good at thinking up new things, so I'm in charge of giving our volcano zip and spark. "I didn't think you'd ever be able to make up your own lines."

"I probably wouldn't have, except that you did it, and it worked. And I knew the scene would be better if I said something right then," she says. "It was funny because when I made those lines up, I felt like . . . you for a minute."

I wonder if my feelings are going to get hurt right then, but I can't stop myself from asking. "Because I messed up?"

"No—not that!" she says. "It's because I felt . . . free. That must be the way you feel all the time. Free to . . . I don't know . . . come up with different stuff. Not be the same as everyone else. Being perfect is so . . . boring."

I was right! I think. Because that's what I thought when Ellie first came into our class. But I don't tell her so.

"But there're good things about being the way you are,

too," I say. "Everyone likes you. I bet no one ever's been so mad at you that he'd let your pet loose."

We have ourselves a big belly laugh over that.

"Girls," Mr. Mooney says, frowning at us from his desk, "keep it down, please."

"But I don't get e-mails from movie stars, either," she says.

"El-*lie*," Mr. Mooney says in his get-back-to-work-or-else voice.

We roll our eyes and work on making our volcano wild and rocky. Which is a little bit like me. I like it that way, because it means that things will never be boring as long as I'm around. Things kind of erupt all over the place in my life. Sometimes the eruptions are bad, and sometimes they are good. And sometimes the ones that I think are bad turn out okay or even good. You just never know.

OFFICE OF THE GOVERNOR

OFFICIAL INVITATION
FRED DARIA'S INAUGURAL ADDRESS

Hope to see you there,
Mary Margaret!

Turn the page for a preview of

Mary Margaret Meets Her Match

1. Dream On

I haven't beat the waffles yet, but this morning, things are going to be different. This morning, I'm going to show them that I am the queen of them.

It's our new toaster's fault the waffles don't already know I'm the queen. My dad says the toaster has a bad attitude. Instead of popping the frozen waffles up when they are done, it flings the waffles up, which always scares my baby sister Liza and makes her cry. I think the flinging and soaring makes the waffles think they can be free. If the waffles were animals, I'd help them. But they are just waffles.

My dad thinks it's funny. He stops the waffles by putting his hand above the toaster just before they are done, so they rebound off his hand and land right back in the toaster. "Back where you belong!" he says.

My mom thinks it's annoying. She just lets them land wherever and then says something like "They can make cell phones that take pictures but they can't make a toaster that works right."

For me it's a game—me against the waffles—and I try to catch them on my plate. I've almost done it a few times, but the waffles always bump bibble bobble off the plate. I'm not sure, but I think they might be laughing at me, and I hate being laughed at.

So breakfast time is crazy at my house, with Liza busting out crying every time the toaster hurls waffles, and the waffles trying to escape so they don't get eaten, and all of us grabbing at them. All of us except my older brother JT, who doesn't even like waffles.

JT is thirteen and most of the time acts like he's too cool to care. But sometimes he can still be really fun. Like yesterday, when he pretended he was a sportscaster talking about a game, which is pretty funny because he doesn't even like sports much. He even made up a name for the person trying to catch the waffles—plate-ster. "And the waffles are in the air, folks!" he said, using his spoon as a pretend microphone. "The plate-ster goes right . . . but the waffle fakes left and the plate-ster misses completely. She dives for the other waffle and slams into the counter! Oooo! Uhhh! That's gotta hurt!"

"JT!" I said. "You bent my concentration." Actually, I like it when JT does stuff like that, but I wouldn't ever tell him.

This morning, though, JT isn't even watching. He's just staring into his bowl of Cheerios acting like he's mad about something. I check in with my memory to see if there's anything I did to make him mad. My memory says just one thing, and it's not something JT could know about because I got away with it. A few days ago I went into his room when he wasn't there and hid under his bed. I knew I shouldn't, but I just wanted to know what he does in there with the door closed. The answer to that is, nothing very interesting. Or maybe he did do interesting stuff and I just couldn't tell because all I could see were his feet.

Anyway, after a while I started to get the giggles because those feet looked like they weren't attached to legs and I started thinking of them as the Feetie family and making up stories about all the adventures they were having now that they didn't have to listen to the legs. I closed my eyes to take my mind off the Feetie family, and then it was so boring that I almost fell asleep.

I'm pretty sure JT doesn't know about any of that because I was very quiet and didn't crawl out from under the bed until he went downstairs. So JT must be mad at somebody else, which is good news for me.

I put the waffles into the toaster, pick up my plate, and stare at the slots. I concentrate so hard, I don't even blink. I hardly even breathe. I'm ready. Today is going to be the day that I finally do it. The toaster makes a ticking sound as it heats the waffles up. Almost done . . . any minute . . . any second. My muscles are on alert, ready for anything . . . ready . . . readier . . .

POP!

The waffles whoosh by me. My body doesn't wait for my brain to tell it what to do. My arm shoots to the right.

I catch one waffle as it starts to come back down. It lands on the center of the plate. For once it stays there. I flick the plate to the left—too fast! The waffle bounces off the rim, but—lucky me!—it gives a little hop up. I have another chance to get under it. I drop to my knees (ouch!). I shove the plate under the falling waffle—just in time.

"I did it!" I shout. "Look! Look! I did it! Now I can add this to my list of things I admire about myself."

My mom claps and says, "That list must be getting pretty long."

"It is!" I say. "I have them all memorized. There's my fashion style, my recipes for interesting lunches, my poems, my understanding of animals, my cartwheels, my—"

"Humility," interrupts JT.

"I don't get embarrassed," I say.

"Humility, not humiliated," my mom says. "Humility is the opposite of being proud. JT's being sarcastic, but never mind him. I think it's good to have things you admire about yourself."

I give JT a dirty look and start to say more things that are on my list, but right then the second miracle of the day happens. Liza—the crybaby in our family—actually smiles. "Look! She's smiling!"

JT puts his bowl in the dishwasher. "It's just gas," he says.

He wants to spoil my good feeling, but I want to hang on to it. "Even if it is, I still caught the waffles, and that was pretty great."

Way to go," he says in his most bored voice. "You're a regular *waffle wrangler*." Then he looks at my mom like there's a whole bunch more he wants to say to her.

"JT," she says, and she looks at him like there's more she wants to say to him. This time, I know what it is. It's "change your attitude."

At least now I know who JT is mad at, and it's not me. Since it's not me, I ask, "What's wrong?"

"There's a snake in my boot," says JT.

My mom holds him by the shoulders and steers him out of the kitchen. "You'll be late for school if you don't get moving." JT goes without even saying good-bye.

Later, when I leave for the bus stop, I feel happy about the waffles but a little sad, too. I think about that for a minute—what's there to feel sad about? Then I figure out it's because the rest if my day will be boring compared to the *glory* of catching those waffles. *Glory* is one of our vocabulary words. It means "shining achievement." I like that word—*glory*. I also like the word *glorious*, which means "magnificent" and "wonderful."

"Mary Margaret!" my mom calls out our front door.

I turn around.

"I forgot to tell you that I'll pick you up from school today. We have some shopping to do."

I groan. I am not a champion at shopping. Pet shopping is the best, but we've only done that once, when we picked out Hershey, my pet rabbit. Grocery shopping is all right because it's pretty fast and I like to watch the lobsters in their tank.

Maybe it's shopping for new furniture. At least when we do that kind of shopping I get to flop down on all the beds and crank the footstools on the recliner chairs—all of them. My mom said that to me once. "Do you have to try every single one?" And I told her yes. Otherwise how would I know which one is best? And she said that we weren't even shopping for recliners. And then I said that I was just working ahead of the family, just like sometimes I work ahead of the class at school, and that when we did want to buy a recliner, I would know exactly which one to buy. And after that, she didn't say anything.

"What kind of shopping?" I yell.

"Clothes shopping," she says.

I hang my head and start walking again toward the bus stop. Clothes shopping is the worst kind of shopping of all! I hate clothes shopping because all my mom and me do is fight, fight, fight.

"It'll be fun!" she yells.

"About as fun as getting a shot on a sunburned arm," I say to the sidewalk. I know she can't hear me, but she must be squinting hard enough to read my mind, even though I'm a block away from her.

"Hippopotamus!" she shouts.

I spin around, zippety fast. "We're going shopping for a *hippopotamus*?"

"No! I said, 'I PROMISE!'"

I slump away. I've never shopped for a hippopotamus before. For a second, I had thought that shopping really would be fun.

Once I get on the bus, things get better for me again. I tell my best friend Andy all about how I caught the waffles. And once I'm at school, I tell my friend Ellie about it, too, only this time I act it out. Ellie and I were in a play together once, so I have a lot of practice at acting. I do such a good job of acting it out that pretty soon everybody is watching me and laughing.

Then my teacher, Mr. Mooney, comes into the classroom and I think he's going to be mad at me because I have this teeny problem about not being able to stay in my seat. And we have had a few little chats about that. Instead, he asks me to do it again so he can see. Everyone applauds and then Mr. Mooney says, "Okay, class, now it really is time to get to work," and so we all do. But still, starting the day like that was a happiness, and I forget all about the shopping trip.

The first thing we do is take our math test. It's the kind of test where you have to see how many problems you can get done in four minutes. We do these every Friday, which today is. The very first time I took the test, I got all one hundred problems done, so I thought I'd passed the test. I even thought I might be a math whiz! But then Mr. Mooney said the answers all have to be *right*, which I didn't think was fair because it's like taking two tests at once—one for how fast you are and one for how good you are.

Mr. Mooney says to practice every day after school. I would rather help my rabbit Hershey practice tricks. She already comes when I call her and now I'm trying to teach her to play ball. What I'd really like is a dog, but my dad is allergic to animal fur so instead we got a rabbit and she stays outside in a hutch. I don't tell Hershey that I wish she was a dog. Hershey loves me and would do anything for me, but no matter how much she wants to, she can't change into a dog.

"Ready?" Mr. Mooney asks. I grip my pencil and nod, thinking that I might as well just get it over with. "Then you may begin."

Even numbers are my favorite, so I do them first. I make up a little poem about them.

Two, four,
Six, eight, ten,
No other numbers
Make better friends!

By the time I'm done with the even numbers, I notice the odd numbers are scowling at me. Maybe they just feel left out. So I make up a poem about them and whisper it.

One, three,
Five, seven, nine,
They look sharp and mean
But I heard that they are kind!

I start liking the odd numbers a little better and maybe they like me a little better, too, because suddenly they are adding and subtracting themselves in my brain just like the even numbers do.

After the time is up, we correct our tests and . . . I pass! I jump up and do a happy wriggle dance next to my desk. It goes like this: "I passed!"—wriggle my botto, wriggle my botto—"I passed!"—poke my finger up high, poke my finger down low. "Oh, yeah, I passed!"—last botto wriggle and two big hops.

I know that Mr. Mooney is going to tell me, "Please, Mary Margaret, sit down, didn't we just talk about this and you must learn to stay in your seat!" I am so happy the odd numbers and I are friends that I don't care. Mr. Mooney doesn't say any of those things, though. He just smiles, shakes his head, and says, "Today must be your day, Mary Margaret."

He's right. Today *is* my day. Because at lunch, after I eat my lasagna sandwich, Granny Smith apple, key-lime yogurt, and carrot-cake cupcake, I notice there is still something. It's way down deep in the bottom of my bag, under my napkin (which I never take out because I am a very neat eater, usually). I reach in and pull it out. It's a package of Twinkies. Taped to it is a note from my dad. *Happy Double Dessert Day, Mary Margaret!* it says.

Ellie leans over and reads the note. "What's Double Dessert Day?"

"Something my dad does sometimes," I say, pulling open the wrapper. I give her one of the Twinkies.

"Thanks," she says, all happy. She eats it in tiny bites. She carefully wipes her fingers and mouth with the damp towel-thingy that her mother always puts in her lunch. Ellie is a neater eater than I am, but you can't ever be too neat or clean for Ellie's mom. "How does he decide which days are Double Dessert Days?"

I shrug. "He's only done it once before, and that was when . . ." Suddenly I feel a little sick to my stomach.

"When what?"

"Ooh," I groan. "Oh no, no, no. They promised. They promised Liza was *it*!"

"What are you talking about?"

"The only other time Dad packed double dessert was on the day my mom and dad told me they were having another baby."

"So you think this means . . . ?"

"Maybe—but they promised!" I hug my stomach and bend over a little. "Ooooo, I don't feel so well."

McKenzie, this other girl in my class, leans across the table and holds out her hand. "Then can I have that other Twinkie?"

"No," I say, sitting up quickly and stuffing the soft, sweet cake into my mouth. I'm not feeling *that* sick.

When my mom drives up in our minivan, I slide open the door. As usual, Baby Liza is in her car seat, which I'm going to have to climb over like I always do. She frowns her baby frown at me and gives her pacifier a slurpy suck. I just stand there. "Well?" I say.

My mom twists around and looks at me over the top of her sunglasses. "Are you going to get in?" she asks. She has a funny look on her face, like she's excited about something and trying not to smile. How can she be excited about having another baby when the one we've got gets in the way all the time?

I put my hand on my hip and say, "When's the due date?" The due date is the day that the baby is supposed to be born, only babies don't always cooperate. I learned that the last time my mom had a baby.

"Due date?" She looks confused. I guess she didn't think I was smart enough to figure out the clues. Her funny smile. Double Dessert Day. Clothes shopping—for her, of course. For those ugly pregnant-lady clothes.

I close my eyes and sigh. "It's easier on me if you just give it to me straight." That's something I heard in a movie once.

"There is no due date that I'm aware of," she says.

I squint at her, trying to decide if she's telling the one hundred percent truth. "We're not going shopping for pregnant clothes?"

"No. What gave you that idea?"

So I explain exactly what gave me that idea.

And then my mother bonks her head onto the steering wheel and laughs. She laughs so hard that a tear slides out from under her sunglasses and her nose starts to run. She laughs so hard that it's making me mad.

I stamp my foot, which is how I say I don't get what's so funny. "Then what are we going shopping for and why did Dad decide to do Double Dessert Day?"

She wipes her eyes. "I don't know why your father packed an extra dessert. He's just being thoughtful, probably. And about the shopping trip, I wanted to surprise you, but it looks like I'm going to have to tell you now." I can tell she's trying to serious herself up. "Cowboy boots," she says. "That's what we're going shopping for."

"Cowboy boots? For me?"

"Yes," she says. "Cowboy boots for you."

My mouth drops open because this is a big surprise. I've been saving for cowboy boots for a while, but it is taking too long. Partly because I keep buying other stuff with my money. Lately I've been begging for them. Begging never works at my house, but when it comes to cowboy boots, I can't control myself. My mom would say I'm obsessed, which means I want them so much that I can't think of anything else, only those boots. *Obsessed* is her new favorite word. *Exhausted* is her old favorite word.

"Red ones? With pink tassels?"

"Whatever color you think the horses would like," she says. She's smiling. So are her eyes. I wonder how she gets her eyes to do that.

This little chat is not going exactly the way I thought it

would. In fact, this little chat is getting weird. When I first opened the van door, I was ready to be all-out mad about her having another baby and about going clothes shopping. Now I don't know how to be. I don't even know what she's talking about.

"What horses?"

"The ones at the Lazy K dude ranch where we're all going. One of my clients wants to throw a party at the dude ranch, so we're going to take a working vacation. That means I work and everyone else in the family gets to be on vacation."

Pppppt. Liza spits her pacifier out and it falls onto the carpeting. There's an indent around her mouth from sucking on that thing so hard. I pick it up and pop it back into her mouth before she can start crying. "When?"

"Tomorrow. So get in already and let's go buy those boots!"

"Tomorrow! But why didn't you tell me?"

"I thought it would be a fun surprise—at least for you. I told JT ahead of time because I suspected he might not be thrilled. He's not."

"So that's what he's mad about?" I crawl over Liza and put on my seat belt while Mom tells me everything. And then I tell her all about my day—reminding her about how I caught the waffles and telling her how I passed the timed math test and did a happy dance and Mr. Mooney didn't yell at me once all day, even though I was up out of my seat one or two or maybe even five times when I shouldn't have been and double dessert and now even the shopping trip is turning out to be a good thing.

"And tomorrow we're going to the dude ranch," I say. "That's about six good things—no, wait. The dude ranch should count double, so that's eight good things in one day!

"Hey, wait a minute," I say.

"What?"

"Shhh," I say, because I am thinking something hard and I can't do that and talk at the same time. What I am thinking is that this day is too good to be true. If my day were a math problem, it would look like this: catching waffles + passing math test + not getting yelled at by Mr. Mooney + double dessert + getting cowboy boots + getting to go to dude ranch where there are real live horses that I will get ride = a perfect day for me. Which means that none of this is really happening at all. I must be having a terrific dream. Good dreams are fun until I wake up, and then they are just a big letdown. But if I was dreaming, then I'd be getting a horse of my own instead of just going to a dude ranch, so something is rotten here.

Then I know what to do to find out if I'm dreaming. "Mom," I say. "Can I have a dog?"

"No," she says.

That's what she always says. And this time her saying no makes me really happy. Because it means that I'm not dreaming and everything else that happened today is real and true. It is a glorious day and nothing is rotten.

I lean forward so I can shout out my mom's open window. "HEY! I'm going to a dude ranch in my new RED cowboy boots!"

My mom claps one hand over her ear. "Giddyup," she says. But she sounds a little less excited than me. Maybe she needs a red pair of cowboy boots, too.